NOTE TO READER

This is a work of fiction. Names, places, characters, and incidents either are the product of the author's imagination, or are used fictitiously, and any resemblance to actual persons, living or dead, business establishments, events, or locales is entirely coincidental.

THE BACK OF MY MIND. Copyright © 2008 by Steven Payette. All rights reserved. Printed in The United States of America. No part of this book may be reproduced, scanned, or distributed in any print or electronic form without the express written permission of the author.

PROLOGUE

She glanced at her watch nervously; it was four in the morning. Her companion told her to calm down, it would all be over with shortly. Just like the last job, in and out in a matter of minutes. She couldn't help it. She was so afraid of getting busted and their plan falling to ruin. They were crouched in a shallow ditch across the street from the target property, waiting and watching for any sign of life. Finally he said "Now" and they began to crawl out of the ditch. The only sound to be heard in the early morning of the crisp Spring day was their own labored breathing as they stayed bent over, close to the ground. They bolted across the country road and onto the property with their gas cans in hand, always looking back toward the road to ensure nothing was coming. They had watched the family leave earlier the night before and were confident no one was at home, but it always paid to be damn sure of that, and they had learned that the hard way.

They made their way behind the house and stopped to listen, to make sure they were alone. A slight breeze blew across the vast property from east to west.

"Did you hear something?" he asked in a quiet voice.

"No, did you?" she replied in an equally quiet voice.

"No."

They continued on their journey until they came across the oil tank at the other rear corner of the dwelling. He took a penlight out of his coat pocket and shined it in the tank's direction. *Good*, he thought. *It's pretty rusted; the flames should penetrate it quickly.*

"Let's go," he whispered.

Silently, they both unfastened the tops on their respective gas cans and began pouring the contents on and underneath the oil tank.

She ran dry and fastened the top back onto her ancient metal can.

"That should be enough," he mumbled as he put his can on the ground between them and began fishing around in his other coat pocket. He pulled out a matchbook and said, "Get ready." She just nodded. He lit one match and held it up to the other matches. They all caught at the same time and lit up like a party sparkler. He quickly dropped the matchbook at the base of the oil tank and grabbed his gas can. Fuel started splashing all over the ground behind him as they ran back to the other corner of the house. He had forgotten to refasten the cap on his can. A few seconds later, a horrific explosion rocked the ground like a major earthquake.

The tank must have been full, he thought, as they ran away from the front of the house and back toward the road.

Suddenly, all he could see were flames as he screamed the most tormented, blood-curdling scream of his life. She was ten feet ahead of him and also screaming as the fire engulfed him, sending him to the ground in a heap of flames and burning flesh. She didn't know how she did it, but she managed to resume running, faster than she had ever run in her life.

"There was nothing I could do to save him" was the only thought going through her mind as she continued running into the darkness. She never looked back.

CHAPTER ONE

Where It All Began

Ever hear the expression "It's about as fun as attending an insurance seminar"? Those long, lazy meetings one must attend from time and time, that seem to go on and on relentlessly. I was scheduled to attend one this very day, and I wasn't looking forward to it one iota. Such is life when you're a freelance investigator. You have to stay abreast of all the latest investigative techniques whether you want to or not. I may actually be able to stay awake for this one, with having slept for a full eight hours last night. While you're on a case, you get no sleep, and while between cases, you catch up. Not the healthiest way to live, I know, but being an insurance investigator isn't the healthiest of occupations either. Mind you, the alternative being sitting behind a desk for eight hours a day pushing paper would probably drive me crazy. Sitting in a little cubicle listening to the lady in the next cubicle drone on and on about how good last night's episode of whatever the latest reality TV show was. That would without a doubt push me right over the edge.

So here I stand, in front of the full-length mirror in my bedroom, trying to straighten the tie it took me a half hour to find. Not that I'm messy, it's just the opposite. Some say I'm slightly obsessive-compulsive about neatness while others say not so slightly. I just believe that everything has a place and should be in its place. As I detest wearing ties and hadn't worn mine in months, I had forgotten where I left my one and only neck constrictor. I finally found it at the bottom of a dresser drawer along with the cuff links I thought I had lost. Just to be safe, I moved the cuff links to the old Quality Street can I kept in my top dresser drawer for odds and ends. You never know when a set of shiny silver cuff links will be required, though hopefully not anytime soon.

Just as I finished dressing in my suit (the only one I have since I'm a jeans and T-shirt kind of guy), the damn Blackberry beeped. God love the saleswoman for telling me how great Blackberry's are. Get real-time emails, phone calls, text messages, MSN messenger messages, etc. The list goes on and on. I must admit it sounded great at the time, but once you actually have it and people know they can contact you day or night....well....it gets a bit frustrating. The only question I had was "Who would be texting me at 7:00 in the morning"?

As I pulled the device from its holster, I realized I knew it was a text message from the constant beeping. I actually remembered the beeping is for text messages! I wondered how long it would take me to remember the different tones this thing makes. This day just might turn out better than I thought. But then I read the text and realized that thought was just wishful thinking.

William Condon, President of The Balmoral Insurance Company, sent me the following message:

Another fire overnight, 11060 County Road 56, Malone. Insured dwelling went up in flames, no one home at the time, family states they stayed with friends overnight. Get over there ASAP.

That's Bill all right, short and sweet, right to the point. This will be the third fire I've been called to investigate in the last two months for Balmoral. The previous two remain open, and this has become a thorn in my side, given my previous case-closure rate of 95%. While this worried me somewhat, at least one positive thing has happened. I could get out of this monkey suit and skip the seminar.

I got a gut feeling as I jumped into a pair of old, torn black jeans and an Ottawa Senators T-shirt. This fire would resemble the previous two to a "T". The house would have burned to the ground, and the fire would have been overly intense due to the use of an accelerant, specifically diesel fuel. Tim Stokes, Fire Chief for Malone County, would have had his men flood the place and destroy any evidence in the process. I'd be standing around, unable to do anything as I wouldn't get clearance to investigate until the Fire Marshall, John Wakeman, wrapped up his investigation. John, being the thorough man that he is, would take hours completing his part of the job. Too bad John wouldn't produce any conclusive results; he never did in "total loss" fire situations. On top of all that, I got to interview members of a hysterical family who would have just lost everything they own. The fun never stopped!

Both Tim and John had been firefighters for nearly three decades. Tim was then promoted to Chief and, shortly thereafter, John assumed the Fire Marshall position. They both had seen and done it all. Tim was in his fifties now, but didn't look it. He was around 6'1 and 200 pounds of pure muscle. His black head of hair was just starting to gray at his sideburns, and his brown eyes were just starting to show the crow's feet that develop with age. John was also in his fifties and stood around 6'1. He weighs about 210 pounds, has light red hair, and red freckles. He hasn't developed any gray hair.

Dressed and ready to roll, I threw on my trench coat (yes, an investigator wearing a trench coat, what are the odds), jumped in the car, and headed off for the highway. While driving down the 401, I couldn't help but wonder what the motive was for these fires. The two previous fires were seemingly unrelated, happening many miles away from each other, the families residing at the properties unknown to each other. Both families were your average, working middle class households, each with a couple of high school aged, annoying kids. As you may have guessed, I'm not even remotely paternal. That's probably why all of my previous girlfriends sought greener grass on the other side of the street, but I don't wanna get into that. The day is shaping up to be bad enough. The only similarities between the previous two fires were the remote locations of the houses, the fact that both families were not present at the time of the fires, and they were both insured with Balmoral.

I could see thick black smoke billowing into the early morning sky as I turned onto County Road 56. Coming around a steep curve, I saw that my earlier beliefs were true. On the left side of the street sat the frame of a 1930's style farmhouse, I say frame as that was all that was left. Tim and John were both on-site barking orders to their respective peons. A distraught looking couple simply stood by one of the police cars and gazed at the shell that was left of their home. As I parked on the side of the road and got out of my new Camry (which was now covered with mud from the pot hole riddled gravel road), I notice something out of the corner of my eye, something very unlike the previous two unresolved cases.

CHAPTER TWO

The Scene

A white sheet lay on the ground some 25' east of the former house. As we have all experienced from murder mystery movies and the like, I get a tense feeling while looking at the sheet flapping in the slight breeze. Just as I start to walk toward the scene, Mike Rogers, the Malone Police Chief, approaches me. Mike doesn't look like a "typical" police chief. Many police chiefs are large, muscular men, having worked their way up the ranks. Mike stands about 5'10 and weighs in around 155 pounds. He's a rather thin fellow, though not quite to the point of resembling a Holocaust victim. His salt and pepper hair is parted to the right, and his piercing blue eyes tend to capture your attention immediately. At first glance, you would think he was a very distinguished man of about 50 years of age. Unfortunately, once he speaks, you tend to lose the "distinguished" thought rather abruptly. His accent is not one I had ever heard before.

"Mornin', Mr. Samuels," he said.

"Morning. Guess this makes number three."

"I guess so, 'cept this one is far more tragic," he said while nodding toward the white sheet.

"Who or what is under there?"

"No one seems to know. Looks like he or she was caught in the fire. Nothing left to identify, 'cept for dentals if we're lucky enough to find John or Jane Doe's dentist. All of the family's accounted for. They're pretty shook up but holding their own."

"If that's the case, maybe we caught a break," I said. "Could have been "The Torch," who wasn't so lucky this time. Maybe the fire got out of hand and caught him."

"Anything's possible at this stage. The M.E.'s on her way, but I doubt she'll be able to tell us anything; the body is nothing but charred bone now."

"When the first fire engine arrived, Hank Jensen grabbed an extinguisher off the truck and ran toward him, says he was totally engorged in flame and already well passed being able to make any sound at all. Hank's a bit shook up, says he'll never forget the rancid smell."

"It's not something I'd care to encounter, that's for damn sure," I said. "My gut tells me there's something more though, it would be too convenient to have the only perpetrator burnt to a crisp right outside the scene of the blaze. I could be wrong, but I trust my gut after fifteen years in this business."

"You may be right. Only time'll tell," he said.

I was about to comment when a large station wagon pulled into the driveway. The words "MEDICAL EXAMINER" in large letters adorned the tailgate. It reminded me of the station wagon Quincy drove in the "Quincy, M.E." television series.

"There's Janice now," said Mike.

Janice is the head medical examiner for the county. We met several times in the past; we both seemed to be assigned to the same type of cases. You don't normally see female medical examiners in the field, but Janice held her own. She was around 5'5 and 150 pounds. She worked out regularly and had quite a bit of muscle on her. She had hazel eyes and cropped blonde hair, almost to the point of standard Military hair styles. The blonde wasn't natural however, you could see a lot of gray roots. I would peg her at 45 years of age.

"Mind if I talk to the family while you deal with him and John Doe?" I asked.

"No, but take it easy on 'em. They're quite upset."

"You know me, Mike, I'm always professional." I gave him a half smile and a wink. It sometimes surprised me, I could be so nonchalant during stressful times like this, even cracking jokes on occasion. Must be my way of easing the tension.

As Mike and Janice made their way to the white sheet and what lay underneath, I headed over to a distraught looking couple. As I approached, I noticed the woman give me the once over. I always get that when I wear my Goodwill shop wardrobe, which is most of the time. I always tell people I'm here because of what's in my head, not what I'm wearing. From their point of view, seeing a stranger in old ripped jeans, a T-shirt and a black trench coat is probably not what they expect, but they get used to it.

"I never know what to say in these circumstances," I began. "Good Morning doesn't seem appropriate. Balmoral Insurance Co., your insurer, has assigned your case to me. My name is Trevor Samuels." I showed them my license and asked, "And you are?"

The man, who had the slight belly of a 40-some-year-old and a beard with gray flecks, was the first to speak. Not one hair adorned his head. Funny how those that suffer premature baldness always tend to keep hair elsewhere. His voice cracked with emotion. Tears flooded his eyes.

"I'm Peter Lipton. Everything we own was in that house. Everything. Why would something like this happen to us?"

"Everyone who experiences a traumatic event like this asks that very question," I replied. "Whether it be natural causes like an electrical short, or some other cause, your life changes forever in an instant. No one is ever prepared for it. It just happens."

"I just can't believe it," he said while staring at the remains of his house. "Why would anyone want to do this to us?"

"Well Sir, at this point, I usually say there may have been an electrical fault to blame, but given the remains in the field, it certainly doesn't appear accidental."

"I don't understand any of this," the lady beside Mr. Lipton whimpered. "We lead a normal life, no enemies, nothing of any value to steal. It just doesn't make any sense."

"Well, ma'am, I've seen a lot of arson cases in my time and while most are for monetary gain, there are quite a few that are senseless," I said. "Marital discord is common, where one spouse doesn't want the other to get the property in the divorce. I even worked a case where a fellow just couldn't stand the sight of his house anymore due to chronic and expensive maintenance the place required, so he set it on fire. Of course, these situations occur when people are stressed to their limit, and they just snap."

The lady, who I later find out is Peter's wife Marsha, said "There's no discord here, Mr. Samuels, nothing even remotely close to what you've described. Peter and I have been married quite happily for nineteen years."

Marsha had a full head of shoulder-length dark brown hair that curled ever so slightly at the tips. One would think it a wig if not for the blatant part in the middle of her head. She had dark brown eyes, wore no make-up, and was somewhat "plain" looking. She was about 5'4, and I wouldn't even take a guess at her weight. Let's just say she looked to be somewhat prone to the finer things in life, food being one of them.

"I didn't mean to insinuate anything, ma'am, I'm just speaking of my past experiences so you can see you're not alone, things like this happen every day. Sometimes for no reason at all, and sometimes for a reason. That's why I'm here, to try to determine what happened and why."

As you've probably noted, I'm not the most empathetic individual on the planet. Never have been. The way I see it, I hade a job to do and emotions just got in the way.

"Everything we own...clothes...pictures...everything is gone," said Mr. Lipton.

"A claim adjuster from Balmoral would have been assigned to your case this morning and is probably on his way here now. He'll arrange accommodations for you at a nearby hotel and get you some money so you can buy some essentials, clothing and the like," I said. "We'll work closely with the fire department and police to try to wrap up the investigation as soon as possible. That way Balmoral can commence with the reconstruction of your home as soon as practicable."

As soon as I uttered the word "practicable," I heard yelling from behind me. I couldn't make out what the person's yelling, and as I turned around, I saw a look of shock and horror on the Lipton's faces. I turned just in time to see the frame of the house sway away from us and start to collapse in on itself. As the second story collapsed into the first, I noticed someone behind and just to the left of the structure. With all the smoke continuing to billow from the rubble, it's hard to see, but I could definitely see the outline of a person, not very tall and rather slender.

Loud snapping sounds erupted from what's left of the house as it collapsed to the ground. The ground shook as if a minor earthquake trembled beneath us. That's when I hear it, something so...inappropriate. As the firefighters continued to douse what's left of the dwelling, the air cleared a bit, and I saw the source of the sound. Now it's my turn to express disbelief and shock.

CHAPTER THREE

Jesse

Laughter. And not just regular chuckles but full-blown, borderline hysterical laughter. The figure pointed at the ruin that had been the Lipton's house and laughed as if the funniest joke in the world had just been told. To say I was surprised would be an understatement. Just as I was about to approach what appeared to be a fifteen or sixteen-year-old boy, Peter started yelling at him.

"JESSE, GET YOUR ASS OVER HERE! WHAT THE HELL IS WRONG WITH YOU?!"

I turned to Peter and asked who the boy was.

"Our son," he replied. Peter ran to the boy, grabbed him by the collar of his black trench coat and dragged him to where Marsha and I were standing. Marsha had not uttered a word, almost like she wasn't surprised by this bizarre behavior.

"What the hell are you laughing at?" Peter queried.

"That's awesome," Jesse replied. "The whole house is gone. Here one minute and gone the next."

I was beyond taken aback. I wondered if the kid suffered from some mental deficiency, or if he was just naturally morbid. He certainly looked morbid. I'm not really in touch with the youth of today, nor do I want to be for that matter, but I was surprised by his appearance. It looked like he wore eye makeup. He stood about 5'8 and very slender.

He wore torn jeans and a T-shirt with huge lettering that reads "MAKE LOVE NOT WAR" across the entire front. This, coupled with black shoulder-length hair with red patches in it, didn't give one the best first impression. He also wore a black trench coat similar to mine. Mind you, perhaps I shouldn't talk with my black trench coat and ripped jeans. But at least my hair is all one color, and natural at that.

"How can you laugh at this? Everything we own is gone. Everything YOU own is gone. You get it?" his father said.

"I know." He chuckled.

I just stood there and watched the interaction. Clearly something was amiss with this lad. I noticed he also wore black nail polish and had three earrings in each ear!

"What were you doing behind the house? You could have been hurt," said Marsha.

Still chuckling, Jesse answered, "What are you talking about, the fire is out, no worries." Then he turned to me.

"Nice trench, who are you?"

"I'm Trevor Samuels, insurance investigator for Balmoral Insurance Co."

"I'm Jesse," he said as he bowed in front of me. "You see a lot of fires?"

"Quite a few, yes."

"Cool, ever see anyone burnt beyond recognition?" He glanced toward the M.E. and Mike, who were just lifting the body onto a stretcher.

"No, I never have. No point of looking at something when you can't tell what it is."

"I'd love to. I should go ask them if I can see it."

"That's somewhat morbid, don't you think?" I asked.

"Fuck yeah, that's what I love about it, man, it's awesome!"

"Jesse! What's gotten into you?" Peter shouted. "That's someone's life you're talking about!"

"Not anymore," he said with a big grin as he watches Mike and Janice carried the occupied stretcher to the station wagon.

I shook my head when Peter turned to me and said, "I apologize for my son's behavior, Mr. Samuels, he seems to be at the age when anything unpleasant or unnerving piques his interest."

"I understand, it's not a problem. We were all young once" is what I said, but I thought, *How could someone find this situation even mildly amusing?* Either this kid had emotional problems of some sort, or the youth of today has changed significantly from when I was his age.

As Janice pulled out of the driveway with her cargo secure in the back of the wagon, Mike approached us once again and said, "Trev, can I speak to you privately for a sec?"

"Trev"....that's a new one. Regardless, we walked back toward the former house.

"As we originally thought, there were no identifiable features left on the body," he said. "Janice will take dental impressions and maybe we'll get lucky."

"That's what I figured. Well, we have to start somewhere right?" I said.

"True. What's the deal with that kid, what was he laughing at?"

"Hard to say. He seems to think this whole situation is one big joke, even though he lost every possession he ever owned."

"Weird. Maybe he's into drugs or something?"

"Again, hard to say. It wouldn't surprise me. Did you get their statements?"

"No, I'm gonna do that now."

"Ok, I'm going to take a walk around. I'll let you know if I see anything out of the ordinary, and no, I won't touch anything."

"Good. Gimme a holler if anything strikes your fancy."

Mike was a good guy but a bit of a redneck. You'd think he's from the South with some of the slang he slung. He must have watched too many movies.

I turned and looked toward the scene, and it was most definitely a crime scene. This was no accident, given our crispy cadaver and all. Most everything was destroyed beyond recognition. I slowly walked the perimeter of the foundation, looking at all the charred remnants. Nothing really stood out. I saw what might have been part of a stove, another piece of metal that might have been a fridge, I couldn't say for sure. There was no question in my mind that some sort of accelerant was used – I could faintly smell gasoline in the air. Diesel fuel to be exact. I completed the perimeter of the house and then walked back toward the perimeter of the property. This was a beautiful piece of property, wide-open space. No neighbors to bother you, lots of privacy. Of course, that's what could have led to this place being a target for Mr. Arsonist. Same as the other two fires, both at remote locations with no one home. I suppose I should consider that the fires were not related, but my gut instinct told me otherwise. Although, the way Jesse responded, perhaps he set the fire just for shits and giggles.

I completed my tour of the property and, of course, nothing out of the ordinary caught my eye. Mike was just putting away his notebook when I re-joined the group.

"Aight folks, that's enough for now. Thank you for your time and, again, my condolences on your loss. I'm sure Trevor and his team will take good care of you and get the ball rolling," said Mike.

"Thank you, Chief," Peter said. "Please let us know if you need any more information. If the perpetrator wasn't the guy in the field, that means the true criminal is still out there. And if that's the case, we all want him caught."

"You can rest assured we'll explore every possibility, right, Trev?"

"Of course," I replied just as Jesse started laughing again.

"What's your problem now?" his mother asked while staring at him sternly.

"Just think of it," he said, "we get all new shit for nothing!"

Now it was my turn to give him a stern look.

CHAPTER FOUR

Adjusting to the Loss

As if on cue, a white Chevrolet Impala pulled into the yard with the Balmoral symbol on the doors.

"This must be the adjuster now," I said. As we all turned to look in the direction of the vehicle, a very attractive gal got out and walked toward us. She had long blonde hair and deep blue eyes. She didn't wear make-up and didn't need any, her fine features were impressive all on their own. She reminded me of Halle Berry, not just beautiful but drop-dead gorgeous.

"Good morning," she said. We all replies in kind. "I'm Tracy Edwards from The Balmoral Insurance Group. Is everyone all right?"

"Everyone here is fine. There was one fatality and the M.E. has taken the body to the morgue for full examination. We're not sure who he or she was. I'm Trevor Samuels. Bill Condon assigned me to this case. I'm investigating on behalf of Balmoral," I said as I shook her hand.

"Tragic," she said as she turned to the Lipton's. "I'm so sorry for your loss."

How did she know they were the homeowners? Must be the grief-stricken look on their faces. But then, she'd probably seen countless families in this situation and could read their body language like an open book.

"Thank you," the Lipton's said in harmony, except for Jesse who wandered back to the rubble to look around. "We're still quite shaken by everything that's happened."

"That's only natural. I'd be worried if you weren't in shock," Tracy said. "I have a cheque for $1000 for you. You can buy some essentials like clothing and food immediately. I've also booked you a room at the Eastway Motel down the road. It includes a kitchenette with all the usual comforts. The room is yours until your house is rebuilt and fit for occupancy."

The Lipton's appeared stunned. "Thank you," Marsha said as she took the cheque from Tracy. "We didn't think the service would be so....immediate."

"I have personally adjusted many total losses, and I find it best to get the ball rolling immediately. That way the clients are inconvenienced as little as possible," Tracy said. "Well, there's no use standing around here. Why don't you go to the bank and cash your cheque, pick up some essentials, and head over to the motel. I'll drop by later and take your statements if that works for you. Do you know where the motel is?"

"Yes, we do, and that sounds fine, thank you," said Peter. He turned to Jesse and bellowed, "JESSE, GET IN THE CAR!"

"Interesting look on that kid," Tracy said.

"Yeah, he's a unique lad, that's for sure," I said as we walked toward the rubble.

We approached Mike and John, who appeared to be wrapping up their investigation.

"Mike, John, this is Tracy Edwards, the claim adjuster," I said as she shook hands with each of them.

"What's the verdict?" she asked of no one in particular

"Our preliminary findings match those of the previous two fires," said the fire marshall. "I believe it was arson and an accelerant was used. The fire seems to have been started at the rear West corner of the dwelling, also the same as the other two. We have some tests to complete prior to confirming anything officially, however."

"I see," Tracy said as she turned to me. "Were you the investigator on the other two arsons?"

"I was and still am, they're both open and active cases, though I'm not making much headway."

"In that case, can I review your files for those cases?" she asked.

"Certainly, I have them in my car. Why don't we go to the coffee shop on the corner and review them?"

"Perfect."

Mike and John shook our hands before returning to the crime scene to wrap up their work. While walking to my car, I took one last look over my shoulder. As I looked at the ruins, I thought, *I know what my goals are now. I'm gonna get whoever is doing this...and I'm going to find out why they committed these crimes.*

CHAPTER FIVE

President's Meeting

Tracy and I came to the same conclusions after reviewing my files and analyzing the facts of each case. Not only could we not figure out a motive, we couldn't even piece together one common denominator among the three cases. As frustration began to set in, Tracy told me that she's leaving to meet the Lipton's and take their statements. I give her my Blackberry number and asked her to call me when she finished so we could discuss the outcome.

I reviewed the morning's events in my mind as I drove to Balmoral to give Bill my initial (and very limited) findings. House burnt to the ground, little or no hope for any evidence due to the severity of the fire, body burned to a crisp, no motive found as yet and no suspects. What an enlightening report this would be.

It seemed Bill had been waiting for me. His assistant sent me right in to see him.

"Hi, Bill, how's it going?" I asked.

Bill looked like a retired basketball player. He was in his late fifties, had gray hair, and stood 6'4. It was hard to believe someone 6'4 would have a belly, but he most definitely did. Must be the thirty plus years of sitting behind a desk.

Bill's office occupied almost a quarter of the 12th floor of the all-glass, forty-nine story building. The rest of the floor was occupied by his staff. His office furnishings were somewhat modern: a very large mahogany desk, a computer monitor being the sole item upon it; matching chairs on one side of the desk; and a large executive chair on the other. His schedule, calendar, file holder, and radio occupied a side desk.

I couldn't help but to be impressed. Everything had a place and was in its place. The side credenza of matching mahogany construction was also clear of personal effects and files. His files were neatly arranged in file cabinets lined up at the other end of his office, directly to the right of a large conference table. I sat in one of two oversized brown chairs located directly to the left of the conference table. Bill occupied the other chair.

"Not bad, what did you find out?" he asked. Typical Bill, right to the point, no mincing words.

"Well, it's pretty much the same as the Mitchum and Smith losses," I replied. "No one home, house burnt to the ground. Only difference is the body burned to a crisp about twenty-five feet from the house. Looks like the arsonist may have been leaving the scene when things got out of hand. If that's true we may never know why he or she started the fires. Other than that, the cases are all very similar, right down to the diesel fuel accelerant."

"Interesting while also frustrating," he added.

"I feel your pain."

"Do you? I now have three total losses totaling payouts of potentially $1.5 million if all coverage limits are exhausted. I also have a board of directors wondering what's going on. That coupled with a significant drop in our share price, with no signs of immediate improvement, has given everyone around here cause for concern."

"I don't doubt it."

"So what's your next step?"

"Tracy Edwards is the adjuster on the case. She's taking the Lipton's statements now. She's going to call me when she's finished so we can review them. We also reviewed the Mitchum and Smith cases for both discrepancies and similarities.

"I figured a fresh pair of eyes might invoke some aspects of the cases I had missed, but unfortunately this was not the case. Other than that, I'm just waiting for the police, fire department and medical examiner reports. Hopefully, something will turn up during the autopsy and/or lab tests."

"All right, keep me informed of any developments. I have a board meeting to attend, so if you'll excuse me."

I stood and walked out of his office.

Driving home, I passed the Eastway Motel and saw Tracy's Impala parked beside the Lipton's Ford Taurus Wagon. Tracy must still be taking the Lipton's statements. As I was about to leave the

Eastway in my dust, I happened to notice movement out of the corner of my eye. I slowed down and saw someone familiar running away from the back of the motel toward County Road 56, the Lipton's street. I especially recalled the trench coat that resembled my own. It was Jesse.

I checked my rearview mirror and saw nothing behind me. No traffic came from the other direction either, so I pulled a u-turn and headed back toward County Road 56, Jesse, and the Lipton's street.

CHAPTER SIX

Got a Light?

I sped up a bit as I had lost sight of Jesse. Why would he be running back toward his former house? He suddenly appears in view again. He was still running. I slowed to a crawl, all the while hoping he wouldn't look back. Man, could this kid run. I remember the seemingly endless amount of energy that accompanies youth. Funny how the body changes over time.

As I went around the curve immediately before reaching the property, I could see Jesse veer off into his now abandoned driveway. As everyone had left the property, I had to assume the fire department wasn't worried about the fire smoldering to the point of re-ignition. I pulled over on the side of the road before reaching the Lipton homestead. I had hoped to hide the car somewhere, perhaps in a neighbor's driveway, but there were no neighbors.

I walked to the driveway and couldn't see Jesse anywhere. He wasn't around the house or in any of the fields surrounding the property. That only left one place he could have gone. About two-hundred feet behind the house was an old barn. It looked like it could collapse into itself at any time. It had probably been built over a hundred years ago. It looked like it hadn't been renovated or updated since its initial construction. It must be used for storage, or perhaps not at all, as the Lipton's never mentioned having any animals. Unfortunately I didn't see windows either. I decided to sit and wait for the kid to reappear instead of entering the barn and startling him.

If he was getting something incriminating, I would catch him with it when he came out.

Oddly enough there was none of that yellow "CRIME SCENE - DO NOT CROSS" tape anywhere. Most unusual. I couldn't figure out why Mike would deem it unnecessary to do so.

A subtle noise emanated from behind me as I stood between the rubble and the barn. At least I now had confirmation that he was in the barn. I gathered the police didn't find anything when they searched the barn as Mike never mentioned anything. He never mentioned the barn at all.

"Come on, kid," I said to myself just as my Blackberry started beeping. This time it was a deep rhythmic tune, and I knew it was an incoming call as opposed to a text message.

"Samuels," I said as I walked back toward the rubble. The last thing I wanted was for Jesse to hear me.

"Hi, Trevor, it's Tracy Edwards. How are you?"

"Not bad, thanks. You?"

"Well, I'd be better if someone had been home when the crime occurred. I took everyone's statement, but there's nothing of any significance to report. Everything was fine when they left the house. They didn't see anyone or hear anything out of the ordinary."

"That's about what I figured. Did you get a statement from the kid as well?"

"Yes, but all he did was stare at my breasts and answer "yes" or "no" to my questions. Nothing of any substance came out of him."

"Ah, to be young again." I chuckled.

"I think he's just a normal teenager, trying to find himself like all the others."

"Yes, probably. So where are you heading now?"

"Back to the office. I'll wait for the fire department, police and M.E. reports. Hopefully at least one of the reports will develop a lead."

"I hope so. I'm heading home myself. There's not much I can do until the reports become available," I said. I'm not sure why I didn't tell her about Jesse running back home and me waiting for him to appear. Must be that old gut instinct again.

"All right, I'll be in touch if I hear anything."

"I'll do the same. Talk to you later." I ended the call and re-holstered the wireless. I had to smile when I thought of the kid staring at her tits. The audacity of youth. I must admit he has good taste; she does have a great rack. Fortunately with age came subtlety – she'd never catch me looking at the twins.

I walked to the barn and put my ear up against the door. I could hear a faint rustling sound. Curiosity getting the best of me, I decided to take a couple of steps back and just stand there. This was the only door and he had to come out eventually.

My patience came to an end after standing still for fifteen minutes. I approached the door again, this time reaching out for the ancient wooden handle. I pulled the door outwards very slowly and hoped the hinges would be silent. Surprisingly, they were. I shut the door very slowly once I had stepped inside. Luckily this end of the barn was lit. Besides the damp, musty smell, it was pretty much as I figured it would be – some loose hay strewn all over the floor and some old rusty tools on a makeshift workbench to my right. Old boxes lined the far wall at the other end of the building. Other than that, the place was empty.

Just as I was about to say, "Where the hell is he", I heard movement under my feet. *I'll be damned*, I thought. *This place has a basement.* I couldn't see any other doors, be it in a wall or on the floor. I was afraid to move as I didn't want the old floor boards to give me away, so I just stood there, waiting.

After what seemed like an hour, I heard footsteps. They seemed to get softer and more distant as they went along. I looked the length of the barn and noticed a faint crack on the floor in the South corner. I had to strain to see it as there was no light at that end of the barn. *Here he comes, and none too soon*, I thought.

Suddenly, the door in the floor popped open with a loud bang. The kid caught sight of me immediately. Something hung out of his mouth, but I couldn't make out what it was.

"Well, hello there, lad," I said.

He didn't reply or move a muscle. He just stared at me. I learned a long time ago that when someone freezes and doesn't speak it's because they're trying to think of a good story to tell you rather than admit to what they had just been doing.

"Find anything interesting down there?" I asked.

Without a word, he then finished climbing out from beneath the building. With his right hand, he took the thing out of his mouth. "What the fuck are you doing here?" he asked rather loudly. "You tailing me?"

"That's right," I said as I approached him. "I happened to be driving by the Motel when I saw you dart from behind the building like a bat out of hell. I thought it odd, so here I am."

"I'm not doing anything wrong, man. I just needed to get some smokes."

I looked down at his right hand and saw what looked like a Ziploc bag with some sort of label on it. Inside the bag were a shitload of cigarettes.

"I see. Don't you know smoking stunts your growth and can kill you? There are over 400 toxins per cigarette."

"Yeah, Dad, I fuckin' know that, but it's my life, not yours."

Smart-ass kid. As I reached for the bag, he stepped back against the wall.

"Don't touch me, or I'll tell the cops you tried to fuck me."

Now it was my turn to freeze and stare. After 30 seconds, I said, "I just want to see the bag, I'll give them back to you, don't worry." I had to tread very lightly. I wasn't going to become the next "Live at Five" story.

"Why do you want to see it?"

"Because I have never seen cigarettes packaged that way. I promise I'll give them back to you."

"You better," he said as he extended his right arm toward me.

"Thank you," I said as I took the bag from him. Yup, just a normal Ziploc bag full of smokes. I was beginning to think he had rolled them himself when my eyes happened upon the label:

Surgeon General's WARNING

Smoking Causes Lung Cancer,

Heart Disease, Emphysema and

May Complicate Pregnancy.*

He didn't roll his own; he had bought them like this. It suddenly dawned on me that I was holding contraband cigarettes, the ones that were being sold around the country at a fraction of the price of legal cigarettes. The kid probably couldn't buy the legal ones anyway because he was too young.

"Seen enough now?" he asked with his arm still outstretched. As I handed them back to him, I asked him where he had gotten them.

"None of your fuckin' business, man."

"Listen, kid, I'm investigating a very serious crime here. Someone lost his or her life here today, and your parents lost their home and everything in it. You can answer me, or we can go see the police chief and see what he thinks of this situation."

"I bought them from a friend, okay. This has nothing to do with the fire, man."

I was about to ask how much he paid for the cigarettes when something else occurred to me.

"What took you so long to get a package of smokes from the basement? You were down there for at least 20 minutes."

The kid looked at the hole left by the open trap door and then back up at me. He had a very guilty look on his face. When he didn't say anything, I did.

"Suppose we go back down there and have a look around."

"There's nothing down there, man."

"Really? Then it shouldn't take but a minute to check it out."

"If you're smart, you'll just forget about this whole thing."

Now I was intrigued. There had to be something down there.

"Once again, kid, you can show me what's down there, or the police can have a look. They obviously missed the trap door when they searched this place earlier," I said.

"They missed it because all those boxes were stacked on top of it earlier. My dad told the cops no one had been in here for a long time, and they didn't bother to move the boxes to see if there was anything underneath. That's what took me so long, I had to move the boxes."

"They didn't look in the boxes?"

"Yeah, they did, but when they got to the last one, they didn't lift it, they just looked inside it. Once they saw it was all junk, they restacked them and left."

"I see. So, shall we have a look downstairs or call Police Chief Rogers out here again?"

Without a word, the kid turned and disappeared down the hole in the floor. I followed him down a very flimsy set of risers. When we reached the bottom of the stairs, I turned to my right and froze.

"Jesus H. Christ!"

CHAPTER SEVEN

Smoke Em If You Got Em

I stood in what looked like a tunnel dug out of the earth. It was ten feet in length and four feet wide. Good thing I wasn't claustrophobic! The floor and walls were earth, and the ceiling was the first floor plank boards. Jesse used an old oil lantern for light.

It wasn't the tunnel that surprised me, it's what I found in the tunnel. Stacked floor to ceiling were cardboard boxes along the entire ten-foot corridor and there were at least fifty packages of cigarettes in each box. There had to be a thousand packages of smokes down here!

"Holy shit, kid," I said.

"Yeah," he whispered.

"You've got quite the inventory here."

"Mm hm."

"Why do you have so many packages? Heavy smoker?" I asked. I only asked that question as I wanted to hear what the kid would say. I knew he was trafficking.

"They're called cartons, and my name isn't kid. Just so you know."

"Okay, why do you have so many cartons of illegal cigarettes, Jesse?"

"I like to stock up in case the supply runs dry. I wouldn't wanna run out," he said.

"That's the biggest crock of shit I've heard in a long time."

"Whatever, man."

"My name isn't man. Just so you know."

He just glared at me as I surveyed the room.

"So do you sell them to the kids at school or what?"

No response. He just looked at his feet as if they would magically transport him elsewhere.

"You may as well tell me the whole story, Jesse. Better me than the police. And spare me the bullshit, it belittles us both."

I'm sure Jesse thought I would turn him over to the police immediately, or perhaps that I was one of the police, being an investigator and all. Truth be told, I'd found that sometimes not informing the police right away worked out for the best in the end. The more people involved, the more convoluted the case became. Even though I could get into a lot of trouble for not reporting the contraband cigarettes, my gut was telling me to sit tight for now.

"I need the money," Jesse said.

"For what?"

"Life. Video games, movies.....whatever I want. I get an allowance, but it's not enough. Twenty dollars a week doesn't go very far, you know. Anyway, my friend Tom knew a guy that sold cartons for $15 each."

"Okay. I'm with you so far."

"Tom and I figured we could sell them at school for at least $25 a carton. People under twenty-one can't buy them in stores and why should people over twenty-one pay $70/carton. It's a win-win situation for everybody."

Looks could be deceiving. The kid looked like a freak, but the more he talked, the more he sounded like an entrepreneur.

"Then Tom got cold feet," he continued. "He was afraid we'd get caught. He was moving away anyway 'cause his dad got transferred. Before he left, he hooked me up with the supplier. I started saving my allowance, and when I had $80, I bought five cartons. I hung out in the smoking area at school and sold all five for $25 each. I used the $125 to buy eight more cartons. It wasn't long before word got around school and within a week, I had strangers coming up to me asking if I had any more."

"Very lucrative, Jesse."

"Well, eventually I built the business up to what I have stored here. Since it was a big order, my supplier delivered them to me. I couldn't very well hide them in my locker at school any more. We never use the barn, and I knew the basement was already dug out. I came across it when I was looking around the property after we first moved here, and I had my supplier bring them here."

"And your parents didn't know?"

"One Thursday a month, we stay overnight at the Parker's house. We all get together, and all of the old people get drunk. I only go because of the Parker's daughter, Sara. She's smokin' hot. Anyway, when everybody was asleep Thursday, I snuck out and ran back here. My supplier dropped off the smokes around two in the morning, and I moved them down here. I was gonna start selling them tomorrow, but then the fire happened."

"Did you notice anything unusual when you were here at 2:00?"

"What do you mean?"

"Well, obviously the fire happened after you went back to the Parker's, and I got the call at 7:00 this morning. What time did you leave here to go back to the Parker's?"

"I'm not sure. I got back to the Parker's house at 3:30, I looked at the clock before I went to bed."

"How far away is the Parker house?"

"They're over on Van Buren, maybe a 20-minute run. I was fuckin' tired when I finished. I ran all the way home, carried the cases down here, and then ran all the way back. I woke up when my mom started yelling. Judy, the lady that owns the house down the road, called her cell phone and told her about the fire. That was at 5:30 this morning."

"Okay, so the fire started roughly between 3:10 and 5:00. That's a pretty good timeline. This is valuable information for the authorities, you know."

"Oh sure, you think I'd blurt out that I was here from 2:00 to 3:00 stacking cases of illegal smokes? Are you fuckin' crazy?"

"Point taken."

We were both silent for a bit. I pondered the timeline, which could potentially become a major factor as the case went along. We didn't usually get such a short timeline. This may help when, or should I say if, we scare up a suspect or two. Could the fire be related to the contraband? Perhaps a rival trafficker was trying to eliminate the competition? I know it sounded thin, but I'd take any leads I could get at this point.

"So what now? You know the whole story, no bullshit," Jesse said.

"Not quite the whole story. Who's your supplier?"

"Come on, man, um, Mr. Samuels. You know I can't tell you that. He'll never sell to me again."

"My name is Trevor, and he shouldn't be selling to you anyway. Doesn't your age bother him even slightly? How old are you anyway?"

"Doesn't seem to bother him. He never asked how old I was. I'm fifteen."

"Fifteen? Wow, fifteen and making big bucks from trafficking in illegal cigarettes," I said. I wasn't going to say it, but I was kind of warming up to this kid. It's not smart to get into this kind of business, but I had to give him credit for having the balls to do it. Come to think of it, even if he were caught, he'd only get a slap on the wrist. The Young Offenders Act is very lenient. I guess he thought the money was worth the risk.

"Yeah, well, it pays the bills." He sort of chuckled before becoming subdued again. "At least, it did pay the bills."

I stared at him while thinking to myself, this kid may be the best lead I've got should the cigarettes factor into these arsons. Best to tread carefully. I didn't want him to clam up. I'd leave the supplier angle alone for the time being. I could always approach it again if need be.

"Legally, I should report this to the police immediately," I said. "If I don't, it could cost me my job and possibly my freedom."

"Mm hm."

"But I'm not going to, at least not yet. I need time to digest all of this."

Jesse turned his head up so fast I thought he'd get whiplash. "Really?"

"Yeah, but don't make me regret it. And none of these cartons are to leave here, understand? Not one!"

"Yeah, man, Trevor. I get it. Why are you doing this?"

"Because I'm not sure turning you in is the best thing to do at this point. Like I said, I need time to digest all of this new info. So while I do that, the smokes will stay here and the police won't find out about them. Cool?"

"Fuck yeah, of course."

"And I may need more info about this business of yours, so don't even think about disappearing."

"Where the fuck would I go?" he asked.

"I don't know, but I don't need any surprises right now."

"You're the surprise. I had you pegged as an asshole from the get-go. You may actually be aight."

"Thanks, I think. Funny, I was just thinking the same thing about you. Now let's get out of here."

Jesse shut off the lantern, and we headed back up the stairs. When we got to the top, he lowered the trap door and piled the boxes on top of it again. I looked at my watch as we stepped outside. It was 7:30, and dusk was upon us. Time goes so quickly. Too quickly sometimes.

"You go back to the motel and keep this little meeting of ours to yourself," I said as I walked to my car. "I'll be in touch."

"Who would I tell? Hey, gimme a ride back to the motel?"

"No. It's as if this meeting never happened, and if it never happened, I wasn't here. And if I wasn't here, how could I give you a ride?"

"Who's gonna see us?"

"One never knows," I said as I got into my car. Once the car was running, I rolled down the window and told him to go straight back to the motel.

"I am," he replied and took off like a shot down the side of the road.

Maybe he wasn't such a freak after all.

CHAPTER EIGHT

Contemplation

I thought about following Jesse to make sure he didn't double back to the smoke stash in the barn. Today was Friday, and school was out for the weekend, so why would he go back tonight? Having laid that thought to rest, I headed home. It had been a long day.

I replayed the day's events in my head, but my thoughts kept going back to the cigarette development. I didn't know very much about the bootleg smoke trade, but I vowed to find out. I was sure the Internet was full of related information. I also wanted to check out the first two fire scenes again. Although it was doubtful I would stumble across a hidden cache of the tobacco farmers' finest, I still had to check it out. It would bother to no end if I didn't. I'd seen enough "Columbo" episodes to know that the loose ends had to be tied up. There's always "one more thing", but right now my one thing was to go home and walk the dog. He'd been cooped up in the house for over twelve hours and would be anxious for a walk.

I pulled into my driveway and got out of the car. I could hear him barking already. He was sitting at the door when I opened it, his tail wagging like crazy. What a life our pets live. Not a care in the world. They get to walk, play, eat, sleep, and get attention. No worries of any kind. I was envious of him sometimes, but then I thought about how boring such a life would get. No excitement at all. "Ready for your walk, Casey?" I asked him. He just looked up at me as if to say "It's about time." I walked to the basement stairs and got his harness and leash. As soon as he saw them, he started jumping around and barking, same as every other night. At least from the dog I knew what to expect. From this case, I had no idea what to expect.

I strapped the harness onto Casey and clipped the leash onto it. We then headed out the door. I can't remember why I got the dog; I had never had one before. I decided to browse the local Humane

Society one day, and there he was. A tan and black Collie/Shepherd cross with white toes. He was a year and a half old (as best as they could figure) and fifty-two pounds. Kind of small for those two breeds, I figured he was the runt of the litter. I think he appealed to me because he was very quiet, just laid in his pen, and looked up at me while wagging his tail. The dogcatcher found him wandering around a country road one day and brought him to the pound. He had been there for two months, and his time was up. I guess I felt sorry for him and here we were eight years later.

    I live in the small city of Marsden, about twenty minutes from Malone. It's a quaint little village right along the St. Lawrence River, which separates the United States from Canada. I liked walking on the path down by the water because it was tranquil. Luckily, the dog didn't like going into the water. I hate the smell of a wet dog. I found it odd that a web-toed animal like Casey didn't like the water, but hey, different strokes for different folks. The moist sea air of spring infiltrated my nostrils and brought a certain peace to me. After a day like this one, I was thankful for that.

As we walked back toward the house, I couldn't help but think about Jesse. At first I thought he was a freak and perhaps on drugs. I altered my opinion after hearing him tell the cigarette tale. I was pretty certain he was drug-free; he didn't even seem to smoke his wares. He seemed to have a pretty level head on his shoulders. I wondered if I may have done more harm than good by not turning him over to the police. He might be in danger if the arsons were related to the illegal cigarette operation. I hadn't thought of that at the time, though I wished I had. Maybe I was getting a head of myself. The two could have absolutely nothing to do with each other.

When we reached the house, I unlocked and opened the gate to my backyard. Once inside, I removed the harness from Casey and gave him a pat. He could use some more fresh air after being in the house all day. I locked the gate and went back in the house through the front door.

I've lived here for a little over a year. I had always rented but wanted to buy a house. It seemed like a good investment. I hadn't heard of this City until I started searching MLS ads for houses. I knew I wanted to live in the country. I had grown up in the city and wasn't crazy about it. Too many people and too much noise. As I didn't have an office outside of the house, I could live pretty much anywhere. I knew I had to check out what eventually became my home as soon as I saw the asking price. The ad showed a nice two story house that offered a modest 1300 square feet of living space. Built in 1917, it contained only two bedrooms, but they were generous in size. I called the realtor and made an appointment to meet him at the house the next day. I was impressed as soon as I walked through the front door. The house had the large door frames and baseboards that I loved. Older homes have so much character, not like the cookie-cutter architecture we see these days.

The new laminate flooring, paint, windows, high efficiency gas furnace, and central air all appealed to me, not to mention the huge washroom and second floor laundry room. The new Kitchen Aid Natural Gas stove, microwave, freezer and Maytag fridge that were included in the asking price sealed the deal for me. There was also a large, fenced backyard with a covered porch and stone patio. The large outbuilding at the back of the yard was appealing as well.

It was already set up as a workshop, which came in handy when I felt like tinkering with something.

I figured there was something wrong with the house given the modest asking price. The realtor explained that the current owner had resided in the house for thirty-two years but, given her advanced age, she could no longer go up and down the stairs safely. She found a suitable bungalow on the outskirts of town and wanted to purchase it quickly. As such she had to sell this house quickly. Talk about being in the right place at the right time!

I grabbed a bottle of water from the fridge and realized I hadn't eaten all day. I had a cup of coffee at the diner with Tracy, but that was it. I didn't have the energy to cook anything, so I grabbed a few slices of bread, a jar of peanut butter and a knife. I headed into the second bedroom, which was actually my office, and flipped on the computer. I opened the Firefox browser and brought up Google while I ate. I typed "contraband cigarettes" in the search field and received over 100,000 hits.

To narrow the hits, I went back and entered "contraband cigarettes Malone". This brought the hits down to a more reasonable

10,000, but still too many to sift through. I decided to look at the first 20 hits and what I found kept me riveted to my monitor for the next several hours.

I had to admit I was a tad ignorant when it came to cigarettes. Having never smoked, I hadn't paid attention to the news stories about them. The first news article contained a picture of a pickup truck with its bed completely filled with cases of contraband smokes. I was immediately reminded of Jesse's stash; the cases of Ziploc bags full of cancer sticks looked identical. As I read the article, I came to realize this was very big business.

Apparently the cigarettes were manufactured on Indian reservations using top of the line equipment. The manufacturing plants run twenty-four hours a day, seven days a week. It's legal for the Indian population to manufacture their own cigarettes. It's transporting them off of the reserve and selling them elsewhere that's illegal. You'd think a cigarette manufacturing plant running 24/7 to supply a single reserve would tip off the appropriate officials. On the other hand, I was sure there were more details I hadn't come across yet.

Each plant was producing two cases of cigarettes per hour. Each case held fifty cartons and each carton held two hundred cigarettes. That equated to twenty thousand cigarettes every hour of every day! Keep in mind, this was per manufacturing line. Apparently some plants had three or as many as four lines operating at once. The cost to manufacture a carton was estimated at $5. Jesse had mentioned that a legal carton retails for over $70. The greed of the government was rearing its ugly head. I had previously read that tax represented the majority of the price of a package of cigarettes. A $5 product selling for $70. At that price, people who bought their cigs legally were pre-paying their health care.

The article didn't mention how many plants were in operation, but I gathered there were a lot of them. There had to be with the amount of money that could be made. I moved onto the next article and learned that the cases were transported all over the country by "couriers". These people were employed to deliver the cases to the "sellers". They did so using regular vehicles such as pickup trucks and non-descript cube vans.

Many sellers had been busted. They were regular, run of the mill people. The smaller sellers held legitimate jobs, lived in middle class neighborhoods, sent their kids to public school, and filed income tax returns annually. The larger sellers' sole source of income was derived by the sale of their product and, in most cases, they were only sold by the case. The cases were purchased from the couriers for $7/carton, which left $2/carton for the courier. The sellers would then charge anywhere from $15-$30/carton. The sellers held the most risk as they were the front-line people distributing the product to the masses. They also made the most money. Each seller paid $350/case and could earn $750-$1500 for that case. Very lucrative indeed.

Some pictures of the police busts were also online. Huge houses, cottages, boats, luxury cars, ATVs, and the like were all seized when sellers were busted. Case after case of cigarettes were also seized. *Wouldn't Jesse like to get his hands on those*, I thought. All kidding aside, I had no idea cigarette trafficking was this big of a business. It reminded me of drug trafficking operations; I had seen a few of those over the years. Billions of dollars were laundered annually by drug dealers. Could you imagine getting rich off of someone else's misery? This situation wasn't that extreme, only because cigarettes weren't illegal yet.

Jesse had around twenty cases in the tunnel - one-thousand cartons. He probably paid $15 each, which would have cost him $15,000. If he sold them for $25 each, he would make a $10,000 profit. For a fifteen-year-old! Maybe I should have checked to make sure he didn't double back to the barn after I left. With that much money at stake, I was surprised he left the cases in an unsecure barn. Anyone could walk in there and hit the jackpot, if they knew where to look. Then again, where else could he store that many cases? He must have bought and sold many smaller lots before he was able to purchase his current manifest. He had obviously been at this racket for a while. The smart-ass said he needed the money to "pay the bills". He mentioned the normal teen things he wanted, but I made a mental note to ask him why he really needed so much money.

This was certainly an eye opener. There must be many unsavory people in the cigarette trafficking business. I was certain all of them would go to great lengths to keep their operations running. A fire or two would create a good scare for someone trying to infringe on another's territory. I didn't know how or why, but I knew the cigarette operation and the fires were related. I also knew I didn't want to divulge anything to the police at this point, it was too soon. It might be a hunch gone wrong on my part, but I doubted it. My instincts were usually accurate, and they were telling me I was just scratching the surface of this case.

It was now 11:30 p.m., and I was exhausted. I was about to shut down the Blackberry when I thought better of it. I didn't want to miss a call or text. I put the peanut butter away, the knife in the kitchen sink, let the dog in, and went to bed. I needed to get some rest. I was certain tomorrow would be an equally long day.

CHAPTER NINE

The Mitchums

Beep beep beep beep. I reached into the darkness for my Blackberry. As I felt along the top of my nightstand (which was actually an old magazine holder with a flat top), I glanced at my alarm clock - 5:30. No rest for the wicked. I pushed the button that opened text messages as I rubbed the sleep from my weary eyes. After a few seconds the following message opened:

Good morning, Trevor. This is Tracy. I didn't want to call you so early in the morning, so I texted instead. Mike called me late last night and said the police & fire department reports would be available at nine this morning. Talk about speed; it usually takes them several days to produce the reports. I guess everyone involved is working around the clock on this one, and rightfully so. I told Mike we'd meet him at his office at 9:00. I'll see you then.

Finally some good news. Not that I expected much to be revealed that we didn't already know. I debated going back to bed, but two things stopped me. One, I knew I wouldn't be able to sleep anyway. Two, the Blackberry awakened Casey, and he knew he'd get walk time when I woke up.

About halfway into our walk through this seemingly deserted little town, it dawned on me that I had a few hours to kill. As such, I decided to head over to the Mitchum place. The first fire leveled their house, which had now been re-built courtesy of Balmoral.

When we finished our walk, I grabbed a quick shower and put on a golf shirt (at least it had a collar) and a pair of rip-free jeans. I grabbed a V8 out of the fridge, gave Casey a pat, grabbed my trench coat, and headed out. It was 7:00, and the air was fresh and crisp.

The more time that passed, the less likely you were to solve a crime. Witness recollections faded, leads dried up and disappeared (not that there were any witnesses or leads thus far but you know what I'm getting at). That's why I worked on weekends; it was too dangerous to stop for two days. The arsonist could be planning his next fire as I recollected these very thoughts.

I headed north on the highway toward Malone. I would make great time as there was literally no traffic at this hour. Matt and Colleen Mitchum owned a 250-acre hobby farm on Mary St. It was a very scenic location with bare land accounting for most of the property, though the ten acres furthest from the road were all bush. Their newly constructed home was an ordinary three bedroom, two bathroom brick bungalow. The only outbuilding was a small shed located directly behind the east corner of the house. Matt used it to store wood for later use in their woodstove. He cut down his own trees from the bush and chopped them into usable pieces.

Balmoral initially suspected the woodstove as the cause for the fire. At one time, it was said that 55% of all house fires were caused by woodstoves. That's why most insurance companies insist on annual, professional inspections and chimney sweeps for risks with auxiliary heat sources of this nature. The Mitchums made it clear the chimney and stove had been inspected and cleaned about a month prior to the fire. Matt said the inspector at the local Stove Store had given everything a clean bill of health. The inspector confirmed Matt's declaration when the adjuster on the case did a follow-up.

I slowed as I drove down Mary St. as I couldn't remember their civic number. Halfway down the country lane, I saw civic number 453, and it all came back to me. Matt's boat of a Buick Park Avenue occupied the driveway, but there was neither movement nor lights on in the dwelling. They must be sleeping. Both Matt and Colleen worked at the local casino until two every morning.

I decided to wander around the perimeter of the house. It looked very much like the one lost in the fire. I remembered Matt commenting that they wanted it re-built with the same floor plan. I walked to the back of the house and looked over the vast flatland. I didn't really know what I was looking for. I just wanted to have a look around. There was no way I could scour the entire 250 acres looking for a hiding place for bootleg butts, but it would bother me if

I didn't at least check it out. Besides, Mike and his team scoured the entire property at the time of the loss, and they came up empty.

As I stepped off the walkway and headed down the property toward the bush, I heard hinges creak and a familiar voice say "Good Morning, Trevor." I turned to find Mrs. Mitchum standing at the back door in her housecoat.

"Good Morning, Colleen. I hope I didn't wake you."

"No, you didn't. I couldn't sleep, so I decided to make some breakfast. I noticed a car at the end of the driveway but didn't see anyone out front. Since the fire, I try to keep an eye out for anything out of the ordinary."

She looked pretty good in the early morning light. She was a natural brunette with streaks of gray. She also had very fine features. It was almost too bad she was married despite the fact that she wasn't really my type. I preferred younger gals, though not too young.

At thirty-six, I held my own looks wise, if I did say so myself. I wasn't every ladies' idea of the perfect man at 5'10, 165 pounds, with very short, light brown hair and blue eyes, but a few had told me I was a catch. Well, one anyway. My mother. That reminds me of a

T-shirt I saw the other day; it read "My mom thinks I'm a catch" across the front. Sounds like the type of shirt Jesse would wear.

Anyway, I pegged Colleen at around forty years of age. Matt was also in his forties, and he resembled a lumberjack in many ways. He was 6'3, about 240 pounds and had long, light brown hair that was naturally curly. He also had a beard and mustache, both of which were in dire need of a trim. If you slapped a plaid shirt on him and handed him an axe, he'd look just like the lumberjack from the old paper towel commercials. He must have looked out of place when dealing cards at the casino.

"I don't blame you a bit for being cautious," I said. "I'd do the same thing if I experienced what you did."

"What brings you out so early on a Saturday?" she asked. "Has there been an arrest?"

"Unfortunately, no. I heard that the construction of your new house was complete, so I thought I'd drop in on my way into Malone. I didn't want to disturb you, being so early in the morning. I know you work late. How is Matt by the way?"

"He's fine, sleeping like a log as usual. Can I offer you some coffee?"

"No, thanks very much, Colleen. I can't stay. I have an appointment in town this morning. Do you mind if I take a quick walk around though? I know the police searched everywhere at the time of your unfortunate encounter, but I never did. I was hoping my eye would catch something that was possibly missed at the time. I know it's a long shot, but we're kind of at a dead end."

I'm not sure if she believed me or not. For obvious reasons, I didn't want to say I was looking for contraband cigarettes hidden on the property. At least she didn't give me the ole once over. She was used to my casual attire.

"No, I don't mind. We heard about the latest fire on the radio when we were driving home from work this morning. You sure have your work cut out for you. They said no evidence was found and that the fire resembled ours in that no one was home at the time.

"They also said someone died in that fire! Someone they suspected to be the arsonist. It sounded like poetic justice to me. I guess seeing you here wipes that theory out. Anything we can do to help would be our pleasure. We want the people responsible as badly as you do."

"Nothing has been confirmed yet. The body may very well be the culprits, but I have to keep investigating until we know that for a fact."

She stopped to light a cigarette then continued, "Yes, that's the best way to look at it. What if you closed the case and another fire was lit?"

Oddly enough, I didn't remember her being a smoker, and I mentioned as much.

"Oh, off and on. It's so hard to quit. If I had $5 for every time I tried to quit, I wouldn't have to work," she said with a slight smile.

"I know the feeling. I've tried to quit a few times but to no avail. May I ask you for one? I ran out the door so quickly this morning I forgot my pack at home."

"You smoke? I didn't even smell it off you when you were here at the time of the fire. Since I had quit at that time, I was very sensitive to the smell of tobacco."

"Well, the smell of the fire probably overwhelmed the cigarette smell I exuded. It was a pretty powerful smell with all the wood and plastics burning."

"That's true enough," she said as she reached back into the house for something. I had hoped she would bring out a Ziploc bag of butts but no such luck. She had a small black and chrome case and when she pushed a button on its side, it flipped open. Inside were neatly arranged cigs held in place by a yellow band.

"Help yourself," she said.

"Thank you," I said as I took a cigarette and looked at my watch at the same time. "Oh my, I'm going to be late for my appointment. Would you mind if I came back another time to look around, Colleen?"

"No, not at all. Anything we can do to help," she replied.

"Great. Well, nice to see you again, and thanks for the smoke," I said as I began walking back up the walkway toward the driveway.

"You're very welcome, Trevor. Good luck with your investigation. If you get the chance, please keep us informed of your progress. We'd be very interested in any developments."

"I'll do that, Colleen, have a good day."

"You, too."

I looked at the cigarette as I drove back toward the highway. What did I know about cigarettes? They all looked the same to me. I put it in the center console and made a mental note to drop by the motel so I could show it to Jesse and get his thoughts. I would bet it was one of the contraband butts. They would have come in a regular package if they were legal cigarettes. Colleen wouldn't have taken them out of the regular packaging and put them in a special case, what would've been the point? Unless she liked the sophistication associated with a cigarette case, but she didn't seem to be the type of person who would care about something as trivial as that. I didn't know what this meant. Maybe nothing, maybe something.

Jesse sold illegal smokes and Colleen smoked them. Pretty flimsy theory, but it was all I had. I looked at the clock in my trusty Camry. It read 8:30. I doubled my speed on the highway or else I would be late for the meeting. I certainly didn't want to keep the lovely Ms. Tracy Edwards waiting.

CHAPTER TEN

Farmer's Grade

I arrived at the police station at 8:58. Tracy was already in the lobby waiting for Mike.

"Good morning, how are you?" I asked.

"Not bad, thanks, how are you?" she replied.

"As good as can be expected. Where's Mike?"

"On the phone."

She wore a semi-snug white blouse and a black thigh-high skirt. Very appealing. I wondered how many past claimants had been thrown off by her physique. Probably a lot of them. Mike appeared in the doorway just as I finished gazing at the twins.

"Come on in, you two," he bellowed as he headed back to his office. We followed him down the bustling hallway. One thing the police station always seemed to be was busy. Phones ringing and voices coming at you from all angles.

"Have a seat," Mike said before handing a report folder to Tracy.

"The police reports' on top. Fire department's right after."

Tracy leaned toward me so I could see the file. By the look of it, there wasn't much to report. The Lipton's closest neighbor called the police at 5:20 a.m. The police notified the fire department, and they rolled to the scene immediately. The house was fully engulfed by the time they arrived. No one was seen (no one alive anyway), and no evidence was viable. The fire department report contained an analysis of the accelerant. It was diesel fuel, the very same accelerant used in the previous fires. There was one difference though – the diesel fuel was identified as "farmer's grade", meaning it had a red color. It was illegal to sell farmer's grade diesel for use in cars, trucks, and the like, so it was dyed red. It was mainly used for agricultural purposes.

"Farmer's grade diesel," I whispered.

"Yeah, I read that," said Mike. "I called Marshall John, and he checked his files on the previous cases. Both reports noted the accelerant as diesel fuel, nothing else."

"Interesting," I said.

"Does that mean something to you?" Mike asked.

"Not really, no. But why would the first two fires be accelerated by regular diesel fuel and the last by farmer's grade diesel fuel? I'm confident all of the crimes were perpetrated by the same assailant or assailants. Why would they use a different grade of fuel this time?"

"Hard to say," replied Mike. "Maybe they had some farmer's grade on hand that night? Maybe they didn't get the regular fuel earlier in the day when the stations were open?"

"That's a good thought," I said. "What do you think, Tracy?"

"I don't know," she replied. "It's not my department. As long as there's no evidence of arson on behalf of our policyholders, I'm happy. I'll get construction estimates and try to get the re-building process started for the Lipton's ASAP."

"Nope, there's no evidence of the Lipton's being involved at all," Mike said.

"There's some good news for the Lipton's anyway," I said.

"Definitely," Tracy said enthusiastically. "So if you gentlemen will excuse me, I'll give the Lipton's the good news."

"Aight, glad we could be of help," Mike said. "You have yourself a good day."

"And you do the same," she replied as she shook his hand. She then turned to me. "So what's the next step for you?"

"Well, I'm going to talk to Mike for a bit, then head out to the Smith's place. They suffered the second fire. I just want to make sure we didn't miss anything." I shook her hand.

"Sounds like a long shot, but you never know. You may find something. I hope you catch him, if it isn't the guy that's already in the morgue that is. Take care, Trevor."

"You, too."

She left the office.

Well, I was glad her job was proceeding nicely. She could proceed with the claim adjustment now that foul play on the Lipton's part had been ruled out Must be nice. I felt like I was stuck in a rut and couldn't get out, just waiting for the next fire.

"Nice gal," Mike said with a crooked little smile on his face.

"Yes, she is, isn't she?" I said. "By the way, Mike, were all the local gas stations checked to see if anyone remembers selling diesel in a gerry can?"

"Oh yeah, that's one of the first things we did once we were told diesel fuel was the accelerant. Nothing came out of it though. Lots of people put gas in gerry cans for lawn mowers and such. It's not really memorable to the clerks, you know?"

"Yeah, that's true. Thanks for the help, Mike, I'll be heading over to the Smith place now."

"Okay, Trev, I'll be in touch if I hear anything. Make sure you do the same, okay?"

"You bet," I said as I shook his hand and left his office.

I had a stop to make before I headed to the Smith place. I needed Jesse to have a look at the cigarette I got from Colleen. I didn't want to compare it to the ones he had hidden under the barn. If he caught me, he might think I was trying to steal them. What little credibility I had built up with him would evaporate if that happened. I also wanted to ask him about his clientele to see if he sold to people other than his fellow classmates. I didn't know which room the Lipton's occupied, but when I pulled into the motel parking lot, both the Lipton's Ford and Tracy's Chev were parked in front of lucky number 7. I could hear voices as I walked to the door. Peter answered after my third knock.

"Please come in, Mr. Samuels," he said.

"Thank you. How are you doing today?" I asked

"Not bad considering. Marsh and I managed to get a few hours sleep. Jesse on the other hand slept for ten hours."

I could see they hadn't slept very well. Both Peter and Marsha had black bags under their eyes. I could only imagine what it would feel like to lose everything I owned. What a helpless feeling that must be.

"Hello again," said Tracy. "I didn't expect to see you so soon."

"No," I said, "I didn't think I was going to make it here until later today. Since the motel is between the police station and my next appointment, I figured I may as well stop now and see how everyone was doing."

"We appreciate that," Marsha said. "Tracy told us of your meeting this morning. It's too bad no evidence was found."

"Yes, that's a shame. But on the bright side, you can start having the debris removed from your property and get the ball rolling on reconstruction now," I said.

"Debris removed..." Marsha said, then suddenly a tear rolled down her left cheek as her lips began to tremble. I realized I shouldn't have said that.

I was about to apologize, but Peter stopped me by holding up his hand. He then walked to his wife and put an arm around her shoulders. "It's all right, no need to apologize. It'll take us a while to adjust is all. Yesterday's events are still very fresh."

"Of course. How is Jesse holding up?"

"Oh, with Jesse you never know," Marsha replied. "Anger is the only emotion he's shown us lately. Except, of course, for the laughter we were treated to yesterday. He had a good sleep, took a shower, and left."

Left. Okay, maybe I should get over to the barn and find out if he was moving the merchandise. I usually wore my emotions on my sleeve, and I gathered Tracy picked up on that. It was probably the look on my face when I was told that Jesse had left. The look on her face as she stared at me said it all.

"Where did he run off to?" she asked. "Let me guess, to his girlfriend's house? I know teenage sweethearts hate to be separated, even for a few hours."

"As far as we know, he doesn't have a girlfriend," Peter said. "Where did he go, Marsh?"

"I'm not sure. I thought you talked to him before he left."

"No, I didn't. I heard you talking to him in the bedroom. He came out here, grabbed his coat, and left. He didn't say anything to me."

"I told him to clean up after himself when he was done in the washroom. He must have gone to a friend's house."

"Probably."

There goes my gut again. It's the investigator in me shining through. I know I was made for this type of work. God knows I have the persistence and tenacity. I never close a case until I've exhausted every possible angle. I didn't like what I was hearing. The kid was gone and no one knew where he was.

"I best be off," Tracy said. "We'll start cleaning up your property right away. If you give me a list of contractors you'd like to use, I can start getting estimates."

"I hadn't thought of that," Peter said. "The house was already built when we bought it, and we've never contracted for any renovations. We don't know any contractors."

"No problem at all. Balmoral has many approved contractors. I'll make some calls and get things started."

"On a Saturday?" asked Marsha.

"Yes. Time is money to both the contractors and the insurance company. They work seven days a week when there's work. Since there's hardly any work in the winter, they pull double duty spring through fall."

"I must say we've been very impressed with the immediate help and personal, professional service we've received," Peter said. "We've never had a claim before and weren't sure what to expect. Suffice it to say, you've exceeded any expectations we may have had and it's greatly appreciated."

"Thank you, sir, that's what you pay your premiums for," Tracy replied as she headed for the door. "I'm sure we'll see each other very soon, and if you need anything at all, please don't hesitate to contact me. My home, cell, and business numbers are on the card I gave you."

"We will, Tracy, thank you," Peter said.

"Let me know if I can be of service to you as well, Trevor," Tracy added. "Give me a call if I can be of any help to your investigation."

"Thanks, Tracy, I'll do that," I replied. And with that, she left. I turned to the Lipton's and added, "Well, folks, I won't take up any more of your time. The hardest part is over, hopefully, and you can start to rebuild and get your lives back on track. I'm going to work hard to try to bring you some good news about this case."

"Thanks, Trevor, just let us know if there's anything we can do," Peter said.

"Yes, anything at all," Marsha said.

"Try and have a good day folks," I said as I left the motel room.

I got into my car and sat there for a few minutes. Where the hell was Jesse? I hope he was at a friend's house. What if something went wrong? What if he hadn't paid his supplier yet, and the guy was getting antsy? Maybe his supplier decided that a meeting was necessary to remind him of his obligation. Maybe I was getting ahead of myself, jumping to conclusions. You know what I thought? There were too many "maybes" and not enough facts.

I started the car and headed for County Road 56. I had to check the barn. I was surprised Tracy didn't ask to speak to me alone. Clearly, she noticed the expression of shock on my face when I learned that Jesse had left, yet she didn't say anything about it. Another fact to file in the back of my mind for now.

The Lipton homestead appeared to be deserted. I parked in the driveway and headed for the barn at a hefty pace. I practically ripped the door off its hinges as I barged in at full stride and headed for the door in the floor. I lifted it and descended into the darkness. As I reached in the general direction of where Jesse had left the oil lamp, I realized I didn't have a lighter to light the damn wick. I couldn't imagine why someone would build a barn without installing at least one window. It was pitch dark down here. I turned and started back up the flimsy staircase when I stopped mid-riser. Maybe the kid kept a lighter down here, just in case he didn't have one on him when he came to retrieve some stock. I went back to the bottom of the stairs and felt around. Lots of dirt but no lighter. Screw it.

I moved in the direction opposite the stairs. I had my hands out in front of me in case I walked into one of the dirt walls. What I did walk into was cardboard. I felt each case as I walked down the tunnel. No way to know for sure, but I'd say all the cases were present and accounted for. I breathed a sigh of relief.

At least the kid hadn't moved his stash. That was one positive anyway. I turned around and made my way back up the stairs. I shut the trap door and started to walk back toward the main door. Suddenly, I heard a voice outside. I froze and held my breath for a minute, listening intently. I didn't hear another sound.

Slowly, I pushed the door open and looked outside. I couldn't see anyone. I stepped into the light of day and looked around the property. Nothing.

As I headed back to the car, I decided I wouldn't return to the Mitchum place today. I wanted to show the cig to Jesse first. I pulled out of the driveway and headed for the highway yet again. The Smith family lived about forty minutes from here, but I could make it in thirty. When I was done with the Smiths, I would head home and review the facts of the case. Maybe there was a hockey game on tonight, usually was on Saturday nights. I made a mental note to also call the Lipton's and find out if Jesse had returned. Once I knew he was back, I could drop by the motel and have a chat with him. Better yet, I should ask him to meet me at the barn. Better his parents weren't around when I questioned him about the smokes anyway.

CHAPTER ELEVEN

The Smiths

The Smith's was definitely a family that marched to the beat of their own drum. Al (short for Albert) was in his mid-fifties and fancied himself a lady's man. Funny, considering his face reminded me of Mr. Magoo. He was also quite arrogant. In fact, some might say he had the personality of a fried asshole.

His wife of ten years, Betty (not short for Elizabeth), was in her thirties and was an uptight, rigid person. She had long brown hair, which she dyed on a weekly basis, brown eyes, and had never cracked a smile while in my presence. She also seemed to be a very anxious, over-protective woman. A year ago, she nearly suffered a nervous breakdown when her daughter developed "pink eye". I wondered why she would go for a man so much older than she was, especially a man who thought he was God's gift to women. The reason soon presented itself. Money.

I don't know how he made his money originally, but he had a lot of it. At least if you believe what he said. "The stock market has been good to me," he once voiced my way. "I go online, buy and sell shares twice a week, and never walk away from the computer without a minimum $20,000 profit per session," he boasted. I had to hand it to him, he had a knack for making money. And an arrogant attitude to go with it.

They owned a 500-acre waterfront property on the fringes of Malone. Neatly pruned trees lined the perimeter of the property, and the house was 300 feet from the road. You couldn't see the house from the road because of all the trees and foliage. The house itself must have been worth at least $800,000. It was a five thousand square foot, two-story eyesore, however. Even though the front porch pillars and miniature water fountain added some distinction to the front of the house, they had rebuilt the house using bright yellow vinyl siding! Just goes to show money and taste do not go hand in hand. I hope they wanted a unique looking house because that's exactly what they had.

There was only one other building on the property. It was a one thousand square foot, one story, yellow siding clad workshop. This building housed Al's assembled model train sets. I had never been inside the building, but apparently, it was quite the railway extravaganza. The building was immediately to the left of the triple car garage attached to the house, and there was an underground tunnel that connected it to the house. The tunnel was built so Al could access the workshop without having to go outside in bad weather.

Surprisingly, their two teenage children were quite down to earth. Sixteen-year-old Jessica was in grade eleven at the local public school and spent most of her free time at a nearby horse ranch. She owned a $25,000 thoroughbred (bought by Daddy of course) and was training him for competition. Fourteen-year-old Thomas also went to public school and was a video game fanatic. When not in school, he could be found playing games on his 65-inch plasma television. He stood 5'8, was also quite slender, and seemed to be a jeans and T-shirt kinda guy. He had short blonde hair of no particular style and blue eyes, quite the opposite of his sister. I wonder if perhaps the Smith children had different fathers because their physical features were so different, what with Jessica's dark brown eyes and hair and Thomas' blond hair and blue eyes.

I drove up Mockingbird Lane to number 5759, home of the Smiths. I made my way up the meandering driveway and parked next to the fountain. Al happened to be standing in front of the fountain doing nothing in particular.

"Good afternoon, Al," I said as I exited the car.
"Hello. What brings you by unannounced?" he replied. Al had the kind of personality that got me defensive as soon as he spoke.
"I was in the neighborhood on a case and thought I'd drop by and see how everything was going."
"Still working for a living?" He chuckled.

Okay, let's wrap this up and get out of here before I say something I shouldn't.

"Oh yeah, no change there. I'll work until I drop."

"What a shame," he said while giving me the once over, as he did every other time we had met. "I see you still buy your clothes from the finest tailor in town."

With a smile on my face, I replied, "With my kind of job, it pays to be comfortable. You never know where a lead will take you." Of course, I was really thinking how nice it would be to punch him in the face. "So how are things going, all recovered from the fire and rebuild?"

"Yes, I sure am. Once the house was rebuilt, we hired some first class decorators. They took care of everything. Betty worked closely with them, and there wasn't much discomfort. Of course, how could there be when you stay in the penthouse at the best hotel in town during reconstruction. Cost me a bundle, but I'm worth it."

Everything with Al was "I", never "we". I started feeling the pockets of my trench coat like I was looking for something. He eyed me strangely and said, "You have termites or something?"

"No, I'm just looking for my smokes. I hope I didn't lose them," I replied. "Would you happen to have one?"

"Christ no, I don't smoke. It's a filthy habit. I have too much to live for."

"That's too bad. I want to quit, but I don't have the willpower. Maybe Betty has one?"

"You actually think I'd let anyone smoke here? What's wrong with you?" He bellowed. "This household is smoke-free and always will be. I'm a strong person, as is the family. We're not so weak that we need a crutch to help us get through the day." Finally a "we" instead of "I".

"Oh well, I can wait," I said. I wondered if my face was getting red; it felt hot. I hoped not because I didn't want to give him the satisfaction of thinking he could get to me. "So how is everyone?"

"I told you, everything's fine here," he said.

"That's good to hear. Say, I heard you have one hell of a train set. I'd love to see it."

"Yes, I certainly do, but it's off limits. I don't even let the kids touch it."

"Can I see it? I love trains."

"Maybe some other time, I have work to do."

I had no clue what his idea of "work" was. As it was clear I wasn't getting into that building, I decided I'd had enough.

"That's a shame. I guess I'll be off then. Take care, Al."

"Yeah," he replied as he walked up the front steps and disappeared into his yellow sanctuary.

I hope to Christ this was the last time I ever had to talk to this asshole. But, given my luck, it wouldn't be. I got back into my car and headed for the highway. It was getting late in the day, and I wanted to walk the dog and review the case before the hockey game started. I wondered who the Sens were going to play tonight when the now-familiar beep beep beep beep of my Blackberry started again. I turned onto Mockingbird Lane while removing the handheld from its holster. The message was from Mike. This struck me as odd since I'd never given him my cell number.

Hey, Trev, Mike here. I just got a call from Peter Lipton. Their kid Jesse hasn't come home yet. He's been out all day, and they haven't heard from him. Peter sounded quite frantic. Given everything that's happened, I'm not surprised. We have to wait twenty-four hours before filing a missing persons report though. I told Lipton the kid was probably out with friends and that he'd show up eventually. He said he had already called all of his friends, and no one had seen him. I told him to call me if he didn't show up later tonight. He was a bit ticked, but I don't have the personnel to track down every kid that didn't get home on time. I jus' wanted to give you a heads up.

Holy shit. So much for the hockey game. I knew something was very wrong. As I headed back to the Eastway Motel, I wondered why Mike texted me that message. It would've been faster to call me. Yet another loose end to file in the back of my mind.

CHAPTER TWELVE

Missing

I should have trusted the unease I felt when I first discovered Jesse had left the motel room and no one knew his whereabouts. I should have gone looking for him right then rather than just checking his contraband stash. As I sped down the highway, yet again (I think I could drive this stretch of road in pitch darkness, with the lights off, and not miss one curve – that's how often I've been north/south and vice versa on this highway during this case), I could only think of the possibilities. Jesse might be injured, beaten by his supplier, or worse. Alternatively, he might be innocently away from the motel. He might be wandering around somewhere on his own, possibly lining up potential chain-smoking clients. I didn't believe the latter, however, not even for a moment. Something didn't fit in this case. I felt like I was chasing my tail and coming up with nothing. Now I knew how Casey felt when he did it. I was no closer to solving the third arson than I was to solving the first two. And that frustrated me to no end.

So much for getting any sleep tonight, I thought as I approached room 7. When I was about to knock on the door, it swiftly opened. Marsha Lipton stood on the other side.

"Have you seen Jesse?" She half sniffled, half cried.

"No, I haven't, I'm sorry to say," I replied as I crossed the threshold. "Where's Peter?"

"He's out looking for Jesse. Despite all the lip Jesse has given us lately, the one thing he would NEVER do is not check in if he was going to be late coming home. NEVER," she almost yelled. I could see the woman was almost hysterical. Maybe I should slap her? On second thought, bad idea. A slap in the face rarely (if ever) worked out favorably for the slapper. Instead, I took her by the arm and led her to the somewhat worn chair in the living room.

"Just sit down and take some deep breaths, Marsha. This is not helping Jesse or yourself. You have stay calm. You don't want to overreact when Jesse comes home. That would just set him off. I'm sure Jesse is fine and will be back at any moment."

"I hope so, Mr. ...Trevor," she said, looking up at me through teary eyes. "I couldn't go on if anything happened to him. I just couldn't."

"I don't want to hear that kind of talk. I know the fire pushed you to your limit. I also know Jesse being away is threatening to push you further than your brain can cope with right now, but you have to stay positive. If not for your sake then think of Peter. He's been through the same life-altering experience, and he's going to need you. You remember that."

She just sat there, not saying a word. I bent over to look her in the eye. She seemed a million miles away. A second ago, she was ready for the funny farm and now she was catatonic. Christ, now what? Maybe I should call Tracy? She dealt with loss and grief on a regular basis. Peter stormed through the door before I could get to my Blackberry.

"Is he back?" he asked as he stared at Marsha, waiting for a reply.

"No," I said. "He hasn't returned, and he hasn't called."

"Goddamn it, I told the cop Jesse would never run off for this long without at least phoning us! Do you know they won't do a damn thing until twenty-four hours have passed?"

"Yes, I know that," I replied. "Why don't you stay here with Marsha while I look around for a while. You both look exhausted. You should both be here anyway, in case he returns."

"Marsha, what's wrong with you?" Peter asked. He must have realized she hadn't made a sound since he burst into the room.

"Nothing Peter," she mumbled. "I'm just worried is all."

I pulled Peter aside and told him of the events that occurred directly before he returned. I also advised him it was probably best that he stay with Marsha for a while, I didn't think she should be left alone.

"Just make sure you call us if you learn anything, anything at all," he said. "We'll be waiting right here."

"Of course I will, and you make sure you call me on my cell as soon as he returns, or you hear anything at all," I replied.

"I will," he said as he collapsed on the couch. Now we were in total silence again. I used that awkward silence to make my exit.

I was ready to pull my hair out, roots and all. I had never been good at dealing with grief, loss or any of that excessively emotional shit. I investigated facts and reported them, whatever they may be. Where the hell was I gonna look for this kid? I didn't even know where kids hung out these days. Were they still into drinking and having sex in public parks?

I thought about asking Mike to put out an APB for the kid, but I knew he'd only tell me he couldn't and that I was overreacting. I decided to head home since I didn't know where to look for Jesse. I was also certain that Peter had scoured the city thoroughly. There was nothing else I could do. I hoped to receive a call from the Lipton's telling me of Jesse's safe return, and I hoped to receive that call sooner rather than later.

When I pulled into my driveway, I knew something was wrong. Jesus Christ, what else could happen tonight! The back gate was hanging open, neither locked nor latched. I got out of the car and walked to the gate. The broken lock was on the ground below the latch. I picked it up and had a close look at it. It appeared to have been pounded until it snapped, probably by a metal hammer. You couldn't climb the fence as it's six feet high and constructed of solid wooden planks.

I walked into the backyard and relatched the gate. Thanks to the full moon, there was enough light to see the back door of the house. As I stood by the back gate and looked through the open door, I couldn't help wondering why Casey wasn't barking. For that matter, where was Casey? He always greeted me when I got home. Too bad I was so afraid of guns, now would be a good time to have one cocked and ready to fire.

I was just about to walk up the stairs leading to the back porch when a silhouette suddenly appeared in the doorway. My heart leapt into my throat for an instant, but then my initial shock turned into unbridled anger!

CHAPTER THIRTEEN

Lost Becomes Found

Tracy! What the hell was she doing in my house? I was about to ask that very question as calmly as I could when another silhouette appeared beside her. JESSE! I didn't know whether to laugh, cry, or start screaming. Instead, I just stood there staring at both of them.

"I just got here myself," said Tracy. "Jesse took the card I gave his parents yesterday and called me. He didn't have your cell number, so he called me to find out if I had it. I knew something was up when your face dropped upon learning that no one knew of his whereabouts this morning. I forgot to ask you about that this morning, but I remembered your facial expression as soon as I heard Jesse's voice on the phone.

"I figured you'd be eager to find him, so I told him to stay put and that I was on my way after he told me your address of course. I didn't want to give him your cell number with me not being here, just in case he called you then disappeared again."

"Okay" was all I could think of to say.

"Sorry about the gate lock," Jesse said. "I can get you another one if you want. It was faster to kick it rather than pick it. I would have kicked your back door in, too, but I figured you'd be REALLY mad if I did that. You never heard of dead bolts?"

"Okay," I said as I climbed the steps and entered my house. Both Tracy and Jesse stepped aside. "Where's the dog?"

"He's asleep on your bed," Jesse answered. "Nice dog, didn't bother me at all when I opened the door and came in. I was worried for a sec, but his tail was waggin', so I figured I was safe." He sat in one of the chairs around the antique table occupying the majority of my dining room.

It was still hard to formulate sentences. Of all the places he could have been, my house would have been last on my list. I turned to Tracy and said, "Where's your car?"

"Parked on the street right beside your driveway. Didn't you see it when you pulled in?" She walked to the living room window that faced the street.

"No, but then I was pretty preoccupied, so I'm not surprised I didn't see it." My anger was subsiding.

"Well, it's still out there." She kind of chuckled as she walked into the dining room and sat down on the chair next to Jesse's. As long as everyone was sitting down, I decided to do the same. I pulled out one of the chairs on the opposite side of the table and had a seat.

Now that I had recovered from the shock of finding the two of them in my house, I actually began to feel relieved. The kid was all right, I didn't get him hurt or killed by forcing him to hang onto his cig stash. He had scared the hell out of his parents, and me as well for that matter.

"Why didn't you call your parents? They're frantic with worry!" I said while looking the kid in his mascara-outlined eyes.

"I figured they'd probably sleep most of the day 'cause of the fire and all," he replied.

Leave it to a teenager not to think of what would run through a parent's head when they thought their child was missing. God, listen to me. Maybe I had some paternal instincts after all, though I still doubted it.

"I was going to have him call his parents, but then we saw you pull into the driveway," Tracy said.

"Call them now, please," I asked of Jesse.

"Okay, sure," he said as he got up and walked into the living room to retrieve my cordless phone. He dialed the number as he stood in front of the TV watching the hockey game. A short time later, he ended the call and said, "No answer. See, I told you they're sleeping."

"They're not sleeping," I said, sounding a bit irritated. "They've probably gone out to look for you. You've scared the hell out of them."

"Oh," he said as he sat on the couch and resumed watching the game.

I can't believe this. The little bastard scares the shit out of me, his parents even more, and here he is. Nice and calm as could be after breaking into my house. Just sitting here watching the game. Unbelievable! Why the hell did he come here anyway?

"Hey," I said in his general direction. "Why didn't you go back to the motel and get my number off the card I gave your parents?"

Without even looking away from the television, he said, "I didn't know they had your card."

"You could have asked them if they had my card," I said sarcastically.

"Yeah. I could've, I guess," he replied.

I looked at Tracy, and she gave me a half-smirk and shrugged her shoulders. She must be familiar with the way teenagers think. She didn't seem surprised at all.

"Well, my job is done," Tracy said after a minute of silence. "Nice place you have here. Must be nice to live so close to the water."

"Uh, yeah, it is...and thanks," I mumbled. My mind was elsewhere. "Did he happen to mention why he wanted to talk to me?"

"Nope. Like I said, I got here a minute before you did." She walked toward the back door. "Bye, Jesse," she said in the direction of the living room.

"Bye," he mumbled, never taking his eyes off the television. He didn't thank her for coming over when he called her either.

"Try to have a good night, Trevor," she said to me. "You look like you need some rest. Like I said, if I can be of further assistance..." She just left that hanging as she disappeared through the gate and into my driveway.

I shut and locked the door just as Casey came down the stairs. He stopped at the bottom, stretched his legs, and yawned. Then he sat down and stared at me, his tail a waggin'. *Some vicious watchdog you are*, I thought. I gave him a pat on the head, pushed the dining room chairs back into the table, and joined Jesse in the living room.

I would have him try calling his parents every fifteen minutes until he got them. Maybe then, I could calm down to the point that I could get some sleep tonight. After I brought Jesse back to the motel of course. I turned to Jesse and said, "Now then, what did you want to talk to me about?"

"Can't it wait till intermission?" he asked, again never taking his eyes off the screen. Ordinarily, I would be glued to the hockey game as well, but not tonight.

"No, it can't wait!" I said as I grabbed the remote and shut off the TV.

"Aw, come on man, The Sens are winning."

"Too bad. I love the Sens as much as the next guy, but I sense we have more important things to discuss right now. I have some questions for you, but first I'd like to hear what was so important that you saw fit to break into my house. And once again, don't call me man!"

"Aight, well...uhm...you remember how I said I wouldn't move my sticks?"

"Sticks...you mean the smokes, yes, I remember," I said.

"Well, I kinda need to sell some. See, I haven't paid my supplier for all of them yet, and he's gonna get fuckin' nervous if I don't pay him somethin' soon."

I knew it, I knew it, I knew it. Just as my gut had told me. One of the facts stuck in the back of my mind had resurfaced.

"How much do you owe him?" I asked.

"Not much more. We been doin' business for a while, and he trusts me now. He delivered all twenty cases even though I was a little short. I have to come up with some cream pretty soon or he's gonna come lookin' for me though."

"How much is not much more?" I asked suspiciously.

"Five large."

"Five hundred?"

"More like $5,000."

I thought about it. One thousand cartons at $15 each is $15,000. So he had already paid $10,000. Man, I worry about making the mortgage at $750/month, and this kid is carrying ten-large around in cash.

"So you already paid $10,000?" I asked.

He looked up at me with a surprised look on his face.

"Yes, Jesse, I did some research. I know what those smokes sell for, right from the manufacturer to the seller."

"Cool. Yeah, I paid him ten large already."

"Where the hell did you hide that kind of cash?"

"In the tunnel, where the fuck you think?"

"I should've known. So you'll still have a $20,000 profit once you've sold all the cartons?"

"Yeah, pretty good for a fifteen-year-old, isn't it?" He smiled from ear to ear.

I was still shocked. How could a kid this seemingly immature pull this off? I was also in awe of the tax-free coin he was pulling down, but I wasn't about to tell him that. I knew what we were discussing was illegal. I also knew the consequences I would face should the authorities get wind of this not-so-little operation, but I still felt the key to solving these arsons was tied to the cigarette operation. The last thing I needed was his supplier coming around creating problems though. I felt like I was between a rock and a hard place.

"So you need to sell two hundred cartons to raise the $5,000?" I asked.

"Yeah, for sure," he replied.

"We may be able to work something out, but I want some answers from you first, starting with the size of your territory. There is no way you can unload a thousand cartons at one high school. Not many kids can afford to buy more than one or two cartons at a time, and I'm sure there aren't a hundred kids lining up daily to buy two cartons each."

"You think so, Mr. Investigator? Try standing at the back of the parking lot behind my school after last bell. You can't 'cause of all the other people standing there waitin' for me. They're lined up with money in their hands. What do you think? This is a nickel and dime operation? There are 2,435 students enrolled in that school and nearly twenty percent of them smoke.

"That's approximately 487 smokers, most of them not able to buy them in stores 'cause they're underage. They could pay people of age to buy them legal smokes, but then they wouldn't have enough money for the smokes themselves. And, just so you know, some of my customers buy five to ten cartons at a time and resell them. I always bring as many cartons as I can carry 'cause I know they'll all sell. So what do you think now?"

I had to hand it to him, he knew his stuff and he knew it well. And that's only one school. Kids get bused in from all parts of the countryside to attend the four public high schools in Malone.

"All right, let me ask you this, wise-ass, how many schools do you supply?"

"Just mine."

"Just yours? You expect me to believe you only sell at your school? With all that money to be made?"

"I can't sell at any others," he said with a little pout on his make-up covered face.

"Why not?"

"Aight, if I tell you the whole story, you can't tell ANYONE you heard it from me. Deal?

"Deal," I said. "But try to call your parents first. They should be back by now."

I waited with great anticipation. I had a feeling I was going to get the entire inside scoop, and I wanted to hear every word. After a minute, he hung up the phone.

"No answer," he said while looking down at the receiver.

"They're probably still looking for you with God only knows what thoughts running through their minds," I said. "All right, start from the beginning."

"You sure you can handle it?" he asked smugly.

"I can handle anything you've got and then some," I said as I stared into his eyes once more.

CHAPTER FOURTEEN

The Background

"I'm hungry," Jesse said.

"What do you like to eat?" I replied. I realized I was hungry, too. I hadn't eaten anything since the V8 that morning.

"Pizza."

"Fine." I went into the kitchen for the menu of the local pizza place. I brought it into the living room and handed it to Jesse. "Here, order what you want, they deliver. You know my address. I have to use the washroom."

While I was in the washroom, I heard him order an extra-large combination with double cheese and four cans of soda. Man, he must be really hungry. There went my diet. I'd lost eighty pounds over the last seven months and was kind of fussy about what I ate. Oh well, what the hell. I had barely eaten over the last two days, a little pizza wouldn't hurt.

Then I remembered why I lost the eighty pounds. The excruciating pain of kidney stones brought on by a poor diet, at least according to my doctor of eighteen years. I sure as hell didn't want those coming back. But then again, moderation was the key. I loved pizza and hadn't had any in over seven months. I could afford to indulge in a few calories.

I returned, sat across from Jesse and said, "We have some time before the pizza gets here. Time to fill me in."

"Okay. Do you have a map of this area?"

"Of Marsden and Malone?"

"Of the entire township."

I thought about that for a minute. "Yeah, I was given one when I bought my car. Buy a Toyota, get a road map. Buy a Cadillac, get a set of golf clubs," I said with a smile. Suddenly, I realized I was feeling much better, probably in anticipation of what I was about to learn. "It's on the wall in my office. I'll go get it."

I brought the map downstairs and spread it out on my mammoth dining room table. The dining room was the biggest room in the house, so when my purchase of the place was finalized, I went and bought a big table. I knew it would come in handy someday.

"Do you mind if I mark it up?" Jesse asked.

"No, I don't care."

"Do you have a pen?"

I fished around in the lone drawer of the microwave stand, found one, and handed it to him.

"Thanks."

I couldn't get a read on this kid. As soon as I pegged him as a freak, he turned out to be quite intelligent. At least as far as illegal activities went. Then I figured him for a wise-ass and now realized he could be polite. He thanked me for the pen and apologized for breaking my gate lock. Must be a teenager thing, he probably hadn't decided if he wanted to be a wise-ass criminal or a polite young man.

Given his actions since we met yesterday, I was leaning toward the former rather than the latter.

I watched as he separated the entire township into three sections. The entire Township resembled a square and when Jesse finished, it looked like a "T" with a short stem inside the square.

"There's the three territories," Jesse said as he stared at the map.

I looked closely and noted that Marsden was in the same territory that Jesse was servicing.

"So you're in one of the small territories?" I asked.

"Yeah, me and a bunch of other guys. I know I'm not the only one."

"It looks like a small territory on the map, but when you look at the whole township, there's actually a lot of ground to cover."

"Exactly. The guy I buy from is responsible for supplying all of us sellers within that territory. I assume the same thing happens in the other two territories."

"So there are three... kingpins that run the entire operation in the township?"

"Yeah. They each have deals with local reserves, and each reserve only provides its merchandise to the suppliers in business with its kingpin. Each supplier then sells to guys like me, and we only sell within our kingpin's territory."

"I see. Has any seller ever crossed into another kingpin's territory and tried to set up shop?"

"I heard of one guy that tried it, but he didn't get very far. I heard he disappeared."

We were silent for a minute, and during that time, I tried to digest everything I'd learned. The entire hierarchy sounded quite efficient, and if everybody played by the rules, there would be no problems. Not to mention the serious coin every member of the hierarchy must have been pulling down. I had a closer look at the map. Even though each arson was quite far apart from the next, they were all within the territory serviced by Jesse. This gave me pause for thought. Perhaps one of the other suppliers was trying to move in on Jesse's supplier and take over his territory?

I pointed at the map. "Why is that territory bigger than the other two combined?"

The doorbell rang before Jesse could answer.

"Pizza guy," Jesse said.

"Good, I'm hungry. I'll get the pizza while you call your parents again."

"Okay."

I paid the pizza guy and was getting plates from the kitchen when Jesse entered.

"Still no answer," he said.

"Really?" I said. "I'm sure they'll be back soon. They wouldn't stay out all night, not when you could show up at the motel at anytime."

We sat at the dining room table and ate while looking at the map.

"Anyway, that territory is much bigger than the others 'cause the kingpin of it started the whole business," Jesse said. "At least that's what I've heard."

"So the kingpin for each territory is responsible for picking up the smokes from the reserves and delivering them to the sellers?"

"They don't pick them up themselves, they have couriers who do that. The couriers deliver the cases to the suppliers. The suppliers then sell them to the sellers, me being one of them."

"Wait a minute. The article I read didn't mention "suppliers" between the couriers and sellers. It said the couriers delivered the cases directly to the sellers, who in turn sold them directly to the public."

"Maybe it works that way in other territories, but not in this one. The supplier I deal with isn't a courier. One time he didn't have any cartons left but said his driver was bringin' in another shipment the next day. Anyway, at your age, you should know better than to believe everythin' you read."

There's the smart-ass side of him coming out again. "Interesting. So what's your supplier's name? What does he look like?" I asked

"His real name? Fucked if I know. He goes by George, but I don't think that's his real name."

"But it could be."

"Yeah, it could be, but I don't think these guys use their real names. I know I wouldn't. He looks like a guy."

I turned and glared at him. "He looks like a guy? That's the best you can do?" I said in a monotone voice.

"I don't know how old he is, maybe in his forties? He's really short and fat."

"You just described a quarter of this township's population. Did you notice anything else about him? A limp, an accent, eye color, hair color..."

"No limp, no accent, didn't pay attention to his eyes, hair color was dark brown I think."

I nodded my head, grabbed another slice, and looked at my watch. It was almost midnight. Where the hell were Jesse's parents? I hope Marsha didn't flip her lid and end up in the hospital.

My thoughts took me back to the chain of command. The chain seemed to go Kingpin - Reserves - Couriers - Suppliers - Sellers - General public. Sounds easy to follow when you break it down that way.

"So that's how it works," I said.

"That's not quite all," he replied.

"Well, then, please enlighten me further, lad."

"Aight, within each territory are kinda sub-sections. At least I think there are. When I first met George, he made one thing very clear. I could only sell at my school, no others. He said the others were already hooked-up."

"What does that mean?"

I figured he already had sellers providing the cigs at other schools, what the fuck else could he have meant?"

"True enough. Why would he care though? As long as you keep buying from him, why would he care where you sold them?"

"Dunno, he never said."

"Did you ever try to sell at other schools?"

"Nah, I had my hands full at my own. Remember, I was small time till recently."

I nodded. There were other places to sell, but I guess schools were the major attraction. Where else could you find a lot of people in one place, especially high school students who tended to have more discretionary income than most adults these days. A shopping mall maybe? Yes, but there would be more onlookers at a mall. Not to mention security. The risk of getting caught was too high. There are probably a lot of private areas to conduct business on a school campus. I couldn't imagine why Jesse could only sell at his school. Yet another unanswered question to file in the back of my mind. If I came across any more loose ends, my head might explode.

"Could it be that another seller wants to supply your school?" I asked. "I know George said otherwise, but maybe somebody's trying to do it anyway? Maybe a guy that supplies one of the other schools has you pegged as a fifteen-year-old punk. Perhaps he thinks you're not strong enough to handle the job?"

He was silent for a bit, probably contemplating this scenario for the first time.

"Anything's possible," he said as he closed the pizza box and sat back in his chair. He put his arms in the air and stretched. A big yawn immediately followed.

This was one fact I wasn't going to file. There are three other high schools in this territory. There was also a university, a college and some private schools. I decided to focus on the high schools.

"What time does school finish for the day?" I asked.

"2:45."

"Do all the high schools finish at the same time?"

"Yeah. Why?"

"I want to meet the other sellers. They may be able to provide some more insight."

"You think they'd talk to you?" He chuckled. "Why would they?"

He had a point, but I still had to try. There was no other angle to pursue at the moment. I could always try to meet George, but I very much doubted that would happen. A stranger showing up to talk about illegal activities wouldn't go over very well. It could also create repercussions for Jesse.

"I can be pretty persuasive when I want to be," I said with a crooked smile.

Jesse rolled his eyes. "Yeah, sure you can."

This kid seemed to underestimate me. I'd teach this kid a thing or two, but not tonight. It was 12:30 on a Sunday morning, and I was tapped.

"All right, please call you parents again. Surely they're back by now," I said

"Aight," he said as he picked up the cordless again.

After a minute, he hung up.

"Nobody there," he said.

What the hell? Well, he sure wasn't staying here overnight. He'd have my basement converted into a tobacco processing plant by the time I woke up in the morning. "Grab your coat," I said, "we're going to the motel."

"But no one's there," he replied.

"They may be back by the time we get there. If not, then you can get some sleep, and I'll wait up for them."

With that, he grabbed his coat and headed out the door.

Casey barked as I headed out the door. Shit, I forgot to walk him.

"Okay boy, we'll go for a walk when I get back," I said to him as I shut the door. I gave the knob a turn to make sure it was locked. I hoped to Christ his parents were back by the time we got there. At least a few hours sleep would be nice.

CHAPTER FIFTEEN

Undisturbed

As I drove along the highway for what seemed like the hundredth time today, I suddenly realized I had forgotten to ask Jesse if he knew what the kingpins looked like. He said he had no idea, that he'd neither met nor talked to any of them. I also asked him if he knew any of the other people involved, anyone at all. He said no.

I opened the console and took out the cigarette Colleen Mitchum had given to me. I asked him if he could tell whether it was contraband.

"Of course I can tell. It's definitely one of ours," he said.

"How can you be so sure?"

"Because the legal cigarette makers put their symbol right below the filter. Ours don't have a symbol, and neither does this one," he said as he handed it back to me.

"You know," I said as I took a glance at Jesse, "I haven't seen you smoke all night. Don't smokers suffer emotional distress when they go without?"

"I don't smoke," he replied.

"What do you mean, you don't smoke? When I caught you in the barn, you had a carton hanging out of your mouth. You said you came back to the property because you needed some smokes."

"I didn't wanna tell you I was sellin' them. You didn't know anythin' about my stash at that point. Truth is I needed a carton for a friend. He was dry and needed some. That's how I make my money you know, one carton at a time," he said. "So now that you know all about the syndicate, can I take two hundred cartons and sell them?"

I didn't know what to say. On the one hand, George would come looking for Jesse if he didn't get paid. At least then, I could get a look at him. On the other hand, he was more likely to send someone else to have a "word" with Jesse.

"I'm not sure that's such a good idea," I replied. "The arsons and dead body may be connected to your current profession and, if so, selling them could provoke another harmful reaction."

"How the fuck do you know one is connected to the other? They probably aren't related at all."

"I don't know if they're related, but it's possible."

"It's also possible I could fart the entire National Anthem. It doesn't mean it's likely," he said sarcastically.

"Point taken."

I surveyed the Eastway parking lot as soon as it came into view. There was no sign of the Lipton's Taurus. I pulled into one of the parking spaces directly in front of their room.

"Let's get inside," I said.

"I think you're paranoid," he said as he got out of the car. "If I don't get five large pretty damn fast, you'll be searchin' for me again. The only difference is this time I will be dead."

I couldn't argue with that statement. We already had one body. Jesse opened the door to room 7 with his key and we went inside. Everything looked the same as it had earlier, nothing appeared to be out of place. Where the hell were these people?

"You must be tired. Why don't you hit the sack, and I'll wait up for your parents," I said.

"Cool," he said as he shuffled into the bedroom and shut the door. He was so tired he didn't even persist with the smoke selling line of questioning. Good. I was certain I'd hear about it next time we met though.

I had to get my mind off the case for a while. I couldn't even think straight anymore. I found out early in my career that sleep deprivation would do that to you. I sat in the old recliner in the living area and flipped on the TV. The sound was so loud I nearly jumped out of the chair. Why had the Lipton's turned it up so loud? Neither of them seemed to have a hearing problem. I muted the sound so it wouldn't disturb Jesse.

I channel-surfed, hoping to come up on some hockey scores on The Score, and I came across a news channel that showed a picture of the Lipton property. I kept watching the screen as the camera panned left to right. They were showing close-ups of all the ashes.

I'm not sure what time it was when I dozed off. I never got the hockey scores.

CHAPTER SIXTEEN

Why Do Things Happen in Threes?

The thunder woke me with a start. I didn't know where I was for a second. When I tried to get out of the chair, I couldn't straighten my neck. Once I had my bearings, I looked at my watch: 9:30. Shit, I didn't mean to fall asleep. I looked around the room, and the profound quiet told me the Lipton's had not returned.

Something was wrong. We had three fires and now three disappearances. Well, I guess Jesse hadn't technically disappeared, but you know what I'm getting at. We only had one body. I didn't want to pursue this level of thinking any further.

The room was void of any movement, and the only sound was coming from the steady stream of rain pelting the front windows. I pushed the drapes aside and looked outside. It was pouring, and there was no sign of the Lipton's Taurus. I stretched my arms and rolled my head around to try to alleviate the neck pain. I quietly opened the door to the room Jesse occupied. He was lying in his bed, wearing boxers that said "Turn me on" across the front. He was sound asleep. I closed the door and headed for the washroom.

After splashing some water on my face, I grabbed an apple out of the tiny fridge in the kitchenette and sat back down in the recliner. What happened to the Lipton's? They wouldn't stay out all night without at least checking in. Something very strange was going on, and I didn't know what to do. Call Tracy and ask if she'd heard from them? Very doubtful. Call Mike and report them missing? It hadn't been twenty-four hours since I last saw them, so why bother. He'd just say they were out looking for Jesse.

Speaking of Jesse, what should I tell him about selling his wares? There was an upside to saying yes, yet a hell of a downside if he got caught. Once you added George and his entourage to the mix, the downside won hands down. Just thinking about it made my head hurt, so I put it on the backburner for later.

Right now, I wanted to review my files. I knew it was pointless, but I couldn't just sit on my hands. I put my jacket over my head and ran out to the car to grab the files. Man, was it ever coming down. When I returned to the room, I sat at the tiny table outside the kitchenette and opened the Mitchum file in front of me. I hadn't gotten a chance to make a file for the Lipton's yet, I hadn't even taken any pictures. I put the Smith file to my right. I always kept my files in meticulous shape. I had to be organized, or I couldn't function.

Stapled to the left side of each file were pictures of all the affected family members as well as the damaged property. On the right side were site diagrams, statements from the family members, and some rough notes I had made when surveying the properties.

I had just started looking at the Mitchum file when I heard a sound from Jesse's room. I looked up just as he opened the door. He walked into the kitchenette, rubbing his eyes.

"Where are my parents?" he asked.

"I don't know, they never came home," I replied. "I just woke up myself."

He sat down at the table. "They wouldn't have stayed out all night without checkin' in. So where are they?"

I wish I had an answer for him. All I could muster was "I don't know, Jesse."

"Something's wrong, isn't there?"

"We don't know that. Don't worry until there's something to worry about. For all we know, they may have suffered car trouble. I'm sure everything's fine. They'll probably be back shortly."

"You said that all fuckin' night, and they still aren't back," Jesse said, his voice full of anxiety. "Something's happened, I know it."

"Jesse, we don't know anything at this point. Just try to stay positive and not worry."

"I don't care."

"Sure, you don't. Typical teen talk once again, always the tough exterior. Too bad the interior was as fragile as glass. I remember that from my own experiences growing up.

"What's with the files?" he asked.

"They're the first two arson cases."

"Can I see them?"

"Sure." I showed him the Mitchum file first. I knew I shouldn't be showing him files containing personal information, but who would ever find out?

"Do you recognize anyone?" I asked.

"No. The property looks kinda like ours though. Nothing around it."

"All three cases have that in common."

He grabbed the Smith file and yelled, "You asshole."

"Excuse me?" I said in my classic monotone voice.

"You asked me for all the dirt on George, and you've known about him the whole fuckin' time."

The lower part of my jaw must have hit the tabletop.

"What are you talking about?" I asked as he swung the file back my way and dropped his index finger on Al's picture.

"That's George," he said.

"Are you shitting me?"

"No doubt about it unless he has a twin."

Son of a bitch! That arrogant bastard was Jesse's supplier! Two of the three dwellings that had gone up in flames were occupied by people involved in the illegal cigarette business! My ole gut was right again, there was no question about the common denominator now. The question then became why. Why did someone set fire to those houses? Was it a warning of some sort? I turned back to Jesse and handed him the Mitchum file again.

"Take a good look at these people. Do you recognize any of them?" I asked.

"No," he replied.

"Take a good look now."

"I've never seen any of them in my fuckin' life, I'm sure of it."

"Does the property look at all familiar?"

"Not at all, I've never seen that place. And before you ask me again, yes, I'm sure I've never seen it before."

Smart-ass again. The Mitchum's had to be involved! There's no way the first fire was just a coincidence, not with the diesel fuel accelerant used in all three cases. Unless it was a red herring. Set fire to a stranger's property to make the motive for the other two fires difficult to determine, try to throw the police off the trail. *I make my money online through stocks*, Al had said. What a liar! I would take great pleasure in having his ass busted.

One thing was certain. None of this would've come to light if I hadn't driven by the motel at the precise time Jesse was running to the barn for a carton. No progress would've been made to date. That, coupled with Jesse being helpful, listening to me, and being truthful with everything I asked him gave me hope these cases would eventually be solved. I turned in his direction and told him as much. The look on his face told me he wasn't sure if I was being sarcastic or not. I wasn't.

"You're not so bad yourself," he mumbled softly, "you just wanna help, and that's cool. But I do have one question."

"What is it?"

"Why are you here?"

"What do you mean? Why am I here in the motel?"

"No, I mean why are you still pursuing this case? You're an investigator for the insurance company. You know we didn't set fire to our house, so why are you still here? Shouldn't the police take it from here?"

"Firstly, there's no doubt in my mind that your family's innocent. I don't, however, know if the Smiths or Mitchums are innocent. It's my job to find out if any member of their respective households had anything to do with the arsons. Secondly, you've been a lot of help to me, and I have a feeling that will continue. We also have to think about the possible disappearance of your parents. Especially now that I know George is actually Al Smith. I don't want the police involved yet, and you should be happy about that. Your stash will remain safe for now. Does that answer your question?"

"Yeah," he said while staring at the floor. "Do you think my parents are all right?"

"Honestly, I don't know, Jesse. I hope so."

"Do you think George...er Al has something to do with them bein' missing?"

"I don't know. I'll find out though, that's a promise."

He just nodded.

"Like I said, try not to worry until we know there's something to worry about, okay?"

"I'm tryin', but it's not easy."

"I know it isn't. I'm going to leave a note asking your parents to call my cell as soon as they get back. I'll also tell them you're safe and that you're with me. That way we'll hear from them immediately, and we don't have to stay here all day."

"Oh yeah, you've left your dog alone for a long time."

Shit, I forgot about the dog.

"That's right, we better get going. Why don't you pack some clothes in a backpack or something, just in case we don't make it back here today. I'll write that note, and we can get out of here."

With that, he got up and went into his room. He returned immediately with a couple of plastic shopping bags.

"I only have a few things. My mom bought me some clothes and stuff yesterday. I never took them out of the bags."

Christ, I forgot he'd lost everything in the fire. I needed more sleep. I still wasn't thinking 100% clearly. "Okay. Do you have everything you need?" I asked. "We can stop somewhere if you need something."

"No, I'm good."

I grabbed a note pad with the words "Eastway Motel" branded at the top of each page. The staff also supplied a cheap pen bearing their name. I left a quick note for the Lipton's and we were off. It was still pouring outside, and by the look of the clouds, there was still a lot of rain to come. Good thing I didn't have any work to do outside today.

Jesse was quiet on the drive back to my place. I knew he was worried about his parents. I wished I could ease his worry, but there wasn't anything I could do or say. I knew I had to bring Mike into this eventually, but I didn't want him poking around too soon.

Casey wasn't happy when we opened the back door and walked into the house. He ran out before the screen door shut behind us. He had tremendous bladder control, but he had reached his limit. Despite his hatred for rain, he ran right to the tree in the backyard and squatted. *Sorry, Casey. When the rain lets up, you'll get your walk, too.* I waited until he finished as I knew he'd want right back in. He never stayed out in the rain.

"Why don't you put your stuff in my office," I said to Jesse. "There's a hide-a-bed in there. You can take a nap if you like."

"Okay. I'm not tired now though."

"How about something to eat?"

"Pizza?"

What is it with kids and pizza. "Sure, go ahead and call. You can watch TV while you're waiting if you want."

"Thanks."

I couldn't stop thinking about Al "George" Smith. I'll make sure that smug bastard got everything he had coming to him. I just didn't know how I was going to get him. My gut told me someone set fire to the Smith and Lipton places over a territory dispute, but who? The "why" was pretty obvious – someone wanted Al and his seller...or sellers out of business. Oddly enough, I hadn't heard of any other recent fires. You'd think if somebody wanted to shut down Al's operation, they'd target all his sellers, not just one. Maybe Al was just getting started and didn't have any other sellers? Possible yet doubtful.

Jesse was well into his third slice and Casey was standing right beside his chair, giving him a little whine every few seconds so Jesse wouldn't forget about him. There wasn't a human food that Casey didn't like. The Blackberry sounded just as I was about to ask Jesse if he was sure he didn't know of any other sellers that dealt with Al. I took the Blackberry out of its usual resting place and hit the button to retrieve the latest text message:

Hi Trev, one of my constables was driving down South Ridge Rd. a few minutes ago, and he noticed a brown Ford Taurus Wagon parked in the middle of a farmer's field. He called in the plate and found out it's registered to Peter Lipton. No one was in or around the car. Do you know why their car would be deserted in a field? I called the motel, but there was no answer in their room. Looks kinda suspicious. - Mike

Man, I was right on the money when I said they might have had car trouble. The only question was did the trouble happen naturally or was it induced?

CHAPTER SEVENTEEN

Dirt + Water = Disaster

South Ridge Rd. was only a mile from Mockingbird Lane, the very street upon which the Smith's lived. Coincidence? I think not. As Jesse and I were driving to South Ridge Rd., I couldn't help but wonder why the car would be left in the middle of a field. If foul play occurred, you'd think the abductor(s) would hide the car, not leave it out in the open. Unless it was a set-up. It appeared somebody or several people working in unison were trying to set-up Al. Given his demeanor, it was easy to see how that could happen. He probably pissed off the wrong person merely by being himself.

As luck would have it, the rain stopped a short time before we arrived at the field housing the Taurus. Three police cars and a crime lab vehicle were parked along the side of the road. I pulled up behind the last car. As Jesse and I were walking through the wet field, I saw Mike get out of the Taurus and start walking toward us.

"See, didn't I tell you he'd come back on his own?" he said with a little smirk on his face.

Yes, I thought, *you're police officer extraordinaire, Mike.*

"Actually, you told his parents that, Mike," I said.

"Whatever. Point being, here he is. Where did you run off to, boy?"

"Friend's house," Jesse said while looking at the car.

"There you go," Mike said as he turned my way. "Why is he with you, Trev?"

"I went to the motel to see how his parent's were doing, and Jesse was the only one there. I got your text message while I was there, and I didn't want to leave him alone. So what do you think happened, Mike?"

"Hang on a sec, Trev. Boy, when was the last time you saw your folks?"

"Yesterday mornin' when I left to visit my friend," Jesse said.

"Did they seem aight to you?"

"Yeah. Well, they were upset about the fire, but nothin' else was different about them."

"Did they happen to mention going anywhere, or if anyone was going to visit them?"

"No, they didn't say anythin' to me. They wanted to get some sleep. They were still tired from the fire ordeal on Friday."

"Do you have any idea where they might be? Do they have cell phones?"

"No, I don't, and no, they don't."

"Okay then. What were you askin', Trev?"

"I asked if you had any theories on what happened," I replied.

"Well, there're no signs of foul play, so that's good. We're not sure why the car is here. There are no other tire tracks in the field, so it was surely driven here, not towed. I don't know what to make of it."

"I don't either," I said as I walked around Mike and toward the car. Jesse walked right beside me.

"Did you look under the sub-floor in the back, Mike? Some wagons have lots of space under the chipboard sub-floor."

"Yeah, of course. Only had the usual things in it. Spare tire, windshield washer fluid, half used container of oil and other fluid bottles you would expect to be under there. Same for the glove box, nothin' out of the ordinary. The keys were in the ignition though. We thought that was strange."

"Is that right?" I asked.

"Yes sir. Now you see what I mean? We have an unusual situation here."

"It would appear so, yes," I replied as I caught sight of Jesse bending over on the other side of the car. As he straightened up, it looked like he put his hand in his coat pocket, as if he had picked something up off the ground. I didn't say anything to him or Mike about it. "Did the crime lab get any prints?" I asked instead.

"Yeah, lots of them. I'm guessin' the majority, if not all of them, belong to the three Lipton's," Mike replied. "But you never know. We may get lucky."

Somehow, I doubted that. "Can I have a look in the car, or are the boys still collecting evidence?"

"No, we're just wrappin' up. Go ahead."

"Thanks," I said as I opened the door and sat in the driver's seat. I felt under the dash, looked in the glove box, got out of the car, and looked under the seats and the armrest in both the front and back. Nothing unusual. I went to the back of the car and had a look in the cargo area. Mike was right, nothing out of the ordinary.

I was tired of showing up at crime scenes and walking away with no evidence. Hopefully, the print lab would come up with something.

"Any word on the M.E.'s report on John or Jane Doe?" I asked Mike as I headed back to my car.

"Nothin' yet, but you know all the tests they do. Usually takes at least two to three weeks to get the results."

And this was only the third day. I turned back toward the Taurus and shouted, "Let's go, Jesse."

"Let me know if anything adverse comes up, will you, Mike?" I asked.

"You bet," he replied.

Jesse hadn't uttered a word since we got in the car, and we were now almost half way back to my place.

"You're awfully quiet. Penny for your thoughts?" I said.

"Nothing to say," he muttered.

"Did you find anything in the field?"

"No."

I didn't say anything at that point; maybe he had been tying his shoelace or something.

"Are your feet wet?" I asked.

"Yeah."

"Mine too. I hate getting soakers. It feels so cold and uncomfortable."

"I really need to get some scratch, you know. George wants his money," he said out of the blue.

"I'm still trying to think of the best way to handle that," I replied. "I think somebody's trying to pin the fires on Al. That doesn't explain why his place was torched though. Maybe he realized someone was trying to set him up, and he torched his own place to throw the investigation that was sure to follow off the rails. Of course I'm only speculating. It would be one hell of a coincidence that diesel fuel was used in all three cases."

"I dunno. I just don't want him coming after me."

"You can sell the smokes. Tomorrow's Monday, so you may as well take some of the cartons to school and start "earning" some money to pay him off."

"Really? Awesome!"

"There's one catch though. You have to let me know when you have enough money to pay him off. I want to deliver it to him."

I looked over at Jesse as I said that last sentence. His head whipped around to face me in record time.

"Are you crazy?"

"Maybe. I want to see if I can get him to talk. He might divulge something that can help the investigation."

"You think that's smart? You might open a can of worms that you mightn't be able to close. Did you ever think he might have taken my parents?"

"I thought of that, but I dismissed it. There's no reason for him to snatch the parents of one of his sellers. No reason at all. At least none that I can think of. And yes, I want to open a can of worms and see what slithers out."

"I hope you know what you're doing," he said hesitantly.

Truth is I had no clue what I was doing. I knew I had to shake things up, and this was the only way I could think of doing it. I had gotten off the highway and was heading down County Road 56.

"We may as well pick up the cartons now, that way I won't have to make a special trip. It looks like you'll be staying at my place tonight unless there's somewhere else you want to stay?"

"I don't have anywhere else to stay," he replied somberly.

Good. That way I could keep an eye on him. As I backed into his driveway, I noted the amount of rain around the property. It looked like they got more rain out this way; there were puddles everywhere. I was going to park the car close to the barn but, given the wet field, I thought better of it. I sure as hell didn't want to get stuck in the mud. I stopped at the head of the driveway and popped the trunk.

"Okay, you go get what you need and I'll make some room in the trunk," I said.

He got out of the car without uttering a word. What would he do if something had happened to his parents? I wondered if he had any other family. I would only tackle that subject if I absolutely had to. I began clearing space in the trunk when I heard Jesse yell "F-U-C-K!"

I ran to the barn and was about to reach for the handle when the door flew outward. Jesse ran right into me.

"THE FUCKIN' BASEMENT'S FLOODED! THERE'S LIKE FIVE FEET OF WATER DOWN THERE!" he screamed in my face.

I just stared at him for a minute then pushed him aside and walked to the door in the floor. He was right on my heels.

"Where's your lighter?" I asked at the same time he was handing it to me.

I lit the lighter and looked down the hole. All I could see was water floating below the third riser from the top of the stairs. Shit, now what.

"This is what happens when a basement is dug out of the earth," I said. "The ground water seeps into it, especially when it rains as much and as hard as it has today."

"I'm totally fucked!" Tears flooded his eyes, and a look of panic crossed his face.

"Calm down, Jesse, let me take a look." I wasn't concerned about getting my feet wet. They were still wet from our earlier walk through the farmer's field.

I descended the stairs slowly. Damn, the water was cold. I stopped as soon as I could turn and look into the tunnel. I didn't want to go right to the bottom of the stairs. I saw the oil lamp bobbing up and down on top of the water. As I turned a little more, I saw the wet cartons, the majority of them also floating. I was absorbing this development when Jesse started yelling from the top of the hole.

"Hey, they're all in sealed bags! Maybe they're okay?"

I turned back toward him, and looking up into his eyes, I said, "They're ruined, Jesse. There's not a chance any of these cartons can be salvaged. There's just too much water."

I turned and grabbed a bag as it floated by the stairs, went back to the main floor, and handed it to him. He turned it over in his hands and saw a bag of wet mess. The cigs were so wet you couldn't tell there were filters. All you could see was tobacco and filter tips.

"Fuck!" He threw the carton down the stairs.

This certainly altered the plan I had formulated moments ago. So much for confronting Al while delivering the money. There was no product to sell to get the money. Even though Jesse never should've gotten involved in anything illegal, I actually felt bad for him. All the work he put into building his "business" was gone.

He seemed deflated and rejected as he sat on the barn floor with his legs up, bent at the knee with his head in his hands. He was obviously crying, and I had no idea what to say. This was a new experience for me, dealing with an emotionally fragile kid who just lost thousands of dollars' worth of stock. He still owed thousands of dollars for it as well. I sat on the floor beside him and said, "It's all right, Jesse, we'll find a way out of this. You'll be fine."

"Thousands of dollars gone," he said through his hands. "I still owe five large. What am I gonna do? Not to mention the profit I would have made when I sold them all."

All I could think of was *Now you see crime doesn't pay*, but I didn't say it. There was no use in adding insult to injury right now.

"I never thought of the ground water," he mumbled. "Why the fuck would someone dig a hole in the ground and not seal it? What's the point?"

"I don't know, Jesse. We've had a pretty dry Spring so far, that's why the hole was so dry. I must admit I never thought of the ground water aspect either. I'm sure you wouldn't have stored the smokes down there had the tunnel been moist when you first discovered it."

"I'm so totally fucked. George/Al will be after me for sure now."

"I won't say don't worry because I know you will anyway. You can't help but worry. But believe me when I tell you that he won't get you, of that you can be sure."

"Like fuck! He could have me taken out while I'm walkin' down the street, or sleepin' at home, if I had a home. You can't protect me every second of every day. Nobody can."

He had a point there. Suddenly everything just got a lot more complicated.

CHAPTER EIGHTEEN

The Second Death

Jesse was biting his nails as we headed back to my place. I didn't have the words of wisdom that were necessary to console him. At this point, I didn't have a clue what my next step would be. I was about to recap the day's events when my Blackberry rang. "Samuels," I said.

"Trev, Mike here. We just got a 911 call from the Smith place on Mockingbird. Betty Smith is holed up in the basement. She said she was folding laundry when shots were fired somewhere in the house. The kids were out at a friend's place, so she shut the basement door and hid under the laundry table; otherwise, she would have gone upstairs to try to get to them. She had her cell on her and called us. She said the shots stopped a few minutes ago. I told her to remain where she was and that we were on our way. Thought you'd wanna know."

"I'm on my way," I said to Mike and hung up the phone. Luckily, no traffic was coming from the opposite direction. I pulled a u-turn and headed back the way we had just come from.

"What now?" Jesse asked.

"Shots fired at the Smith place," I replied.

"Really? Who was shot?"

"I don't know. Mike and his boys are on their way there now. Mrs. Smith called them and said she heard shots being fired. She's in the basement under the laundry table waiting for them. It looks like I'll finally get into that house of theirs."

"Maybe Al's dead! That would get me out from my debt!" Jesse said enthusiastically.

We would suffer a major setback if Al were killed, I needed to question him.

"We don't know anything yet," I said.

"Yeah, I know, but it's possible."

Yes, it's possible. I wished I knew of a way to infiltrate one of the other territories in a timely fashion. I didn't have time to infiltrate one the regular way. It could take months getting them to trust me. First, the body at the Lipton place, then the Lipton's themselves disappear. Now shots had been fired at the Smith place. I didn't have months.

I had never seen so many police cars in one place. I parked on the street as close to the house as I could. I didn't know if the gunman was still in the house, or if he had already left the scene. As such, I told Jesse to stay in the car and keep the windows shut and the doors locked. I also told him not to open the doors or windows for anyone except me. He didn't seem happy to have to wait in the car, but he didn't say anything.

I got out of the car and walked to the house. I was met at the door by a constable I hadn't met before.

"This is a crime scene. Who are you?" he asked.

"Trevor Samuels, Mike is expecting me."

He gave me the once-over and said, "Just a minute" as he grabbed his walkie talkie and called Mike.

Mike's hollow-sounding "Yeah" immediately followed the crackle emitted by the device.

"Guy at the front door, Trevor something, says you're expecting him."

"Let him through."

I entered the house. I knew Mike was wherever the action took place, so I concentrated on locating the action. A lot of police officers stood around, doing nothing. I kept walking until I heard a distant voice yelling my name.

"Mike? Where are you?" I yelled back.

"Upstairs."

"I'm coming."

Where are the stairs? Now that I had stopped to look around, I noticed the weird layout of the house. That didn't surprise me though, considering the owner. I walked into what looked like a family room. It contained a huge TV, three leather sofas, two leather chairs, a leather footrest, a huge aquarium and four floor-to-ceiling bookcases that were overflowing with books. Beyond that room were the stairs. Most houses have the staircase near the front door for convenience. But no, not Al, his had to be right at the furthest corner of the dwelling. I walked upstairs and saw Mike at the end of the hall. I walked over to him.

"He's dead," Mike said.

"Who is?" I asked.

"Al Smith."

Great. The one lead I had was gone.

"What happened to him?"

"Shot in the head at close range. Looks like he was reading a book when it happened. Do you want to see him?"

"No, shot in the head is shot in the head. I would like to see the ballistics report when it becomes available though. Any sign of a struggle?"

"Nope, none at all. He's just sitting in a chair with a book in his lap. We can't move him till the coroner gives the okay."

"Where are Betty and the kids?"

"The kids are still out at a friend's place, I'm not sure where. Betty flipped out when we told her about Al. She started screaming and threw herself on the floor. I thought she was having a seizure or something, just wigglin' around on the floor. The ambulance we brought with us took her to the hospital. Another one is coming for Al."

"That's a shame. Did she get a look at the shooter?"

"I asked her that when she called us originally, she said no. Probably just as well. If she had seen him, she'd be dead as well. Gunmen don't like to leave witnesses."

I nodded. I seemed to be doing that a lot lately. I thanked Mike and headed for the car. Jesse was looking out the window, watching me walk back.

"What happened?" he asked anxiously as I got in the car.

"Al's dead."

"Awesome!"

"Jesse! A man is dead! The only man I could've gotten answers from! Please keep the celebration to yourself."

"Sorry. This is good for you, too, you know."

I looked at him and said, "How do you figure that?"

"Because," he said "now you know for a fact that Al was a target. And why was he a target? Obviously, somebody wanted him out of the way. And why would someone want him out of the way? They want his territory."

"Okay Jesse, in that case, I have but one question for you."

"What?"

"Who?"

CHAPTER NINETEEN

Stalled Before It Even Started

I was spent. As soon as we got back to my place, I took Casey for a short walk and put clean sheets on the hide-a-bed (which was commonly referred to as "Casey's Couch" as he was the only one to sleep on it in years, though I didn't share that with Jesse). Jesse fell asleep as soon as his head hit the pillow. I then crashed myself.

I awoke at 5:30 on Monday morning. Day four on the case, and it felt as though I hadn't made any progress. Actually, scratch that. Every time I made progress, something happened to stop me dead in my tracks. I think that was more frustrating than not making any progress at all. It was still dark outside when I slapped the harness on the dog and ventured out for our morning walk. Poor Casey hadn't been walked for more than fifteen minutes in the last couple of days. He was very excited to smell all the wonderful scents every fire hydrant had to offer.

I didn't even want to think about the case. Every time I did, I reached the same dead end. Three houses burnt to the ground. One dead body with no clue who it was. The two people that suffered the latest fire were missing. Thousands of dollars' worth of contraband cigarettes had been destroyed. The asshole that owned the second house that burned to the ground was shot dead, and his wife was in a mental hospital. I had no information regarding the other two territories that dealt in illegal cigs. And the grand finale, I had a fifteen-year-old kid staying with me, and he was probably in danger. A fifteen-year-old I might not be able to protect, despite my words to the contrary.

The last four days were shaping up to be the most eventful in my life. We'd been walking for forty-five minutes and were almost back home when the beeping started. There could only be one person messaging me at this hour:

Trevor, what progress have you made so far? I'll see you in my office at 9:00 sharp! - Bill

Good ole Bill, I should have expected his message. Now that the weekend was over, he'd want a full report, and I had a lot to tell him. Bill was the one man I could unload the whole story to. He wouldn't do anything until I told him to, and that included telling the police about the cigarette operation. Bill was old-school; he believed in looking out for yourself and your buddies and letting the chips fall where they may. It might do me some good to spill my guts because he might notice a fact that I had missed.

And speaking of the police, a new fact just dawned on me. Mike called me regarding the 911 call from Betty Smith, I went over, and we conversed. Not once did I recall him asking what the motive for Al's murder could be. He never asked what the motive could be for the Lipton's disappearance either. That should've been foremost on his mind, yet not a word. Mike may be a hick with an accent from God-only-knows where, but he had always been competent in the past. This definitely wasn't another fact for the back of my mind. I had to put it on the front burner.

Jesse was still sleeping when we got home. He needed it after everything he'd been through. What's worse, there didn't appear to be any end in sight. I jumped in the shower, shaved, and got a clean pair of jeans out of my bedroom closet. I didn't get too many stares when I wore the golf shirt yesterday, so I decided to wear another one today. One couldn't look too slovenly when on the job....apparently.

When I was dressed, I went into my office and sat on the edge of the hide-a-bed.

"Jesse," I whispered as I shook his shoulder.

"Mmmm."

"You should get up. We have to go out soon."

"School doesn't start till 8:00," he murmured through the pillow.

"I think you should miss school today. With everything going on, it may be best to stay close to home. I have a meeting with my employer this morning, so why don't you come with me? You can take a shower, and I'll make some breakfast. The housekeeper's coming this morning anyway. You'd just be in her way if you were here."

He lifted his head and turned to face me. Squinting from the light, he said, "Why the fuck do you have a housekeeper? You're only one person. How much mess could you make?"

"Yes, I'm only one person, who doesn't like to clean. I also don't leave messes, and neither will you while you're here. That's why Tanya only comes once every two weeks."

"You're unreal," he said as he put his face back into the pillow.

"Come on, Jesse, get up, we have to get moving."

"Fine," he whined and threw off the covers. He was only wearing boxers again, this pair with a happy face on the front immediately followed by "WELCOME" and then another happy face. Very original. This brought about another thought.

"Do your clothes need to be washed? Tanya will do them for you if you leave them in the hamper beside the washing machine."

"Fine," he replied again.

"Are all teenagers this grumpy in the morning?"

"I'm not all teenagers," he said as he grabbed one of the shopping bags and headed into the washroom.

I could only shake my head.

CHAPTER TWENTY

Concentrating on a Different Angle

We arrived at Bill's office at 8:59, which is a good thing. When you arrived late for a meeting, Bill would look at the clock at the far end of his office as you entered. It gave one a feeling of unease. Bill's assistant, Janet, gave Jesse the once over. Finally someone other than myself drew the attention of the fashion police! I can imagine what the look on her face would've been had he applied his make-up this morning. He hadn't yet had time to replenish his stock of cosmetics. I think it was the long black hair with red patches that caught Janet's eye. His T-shirt with "Just Do Me" in large letters across the front didn't help to stop the staring either. I had to smile.

"Good Morning, Janet," I said. "Don't you look nice today."

Never taking her eyes off Jesse, she replied, "Thank you, sir. You may go ahead in. Mr. Condon is waiting for you."

Janet was very prim and proper. She was a petite woman of Asian descent who kept her long black hair tied up in a bun. One thing about Janet, she always wore business suits and a white blouse. She never wore skirts, which was a shame. It's always nice to catch a glimpse of nice legs, which I was sure she had.

"Thank you," I replied as I turned to Jesse.

"Sit out here and please don't go anywhere. I shouldn't be long," I said.

Without a word, he sat and grabbed a magazine.

I walked through one of the double doors that led to Bill's office and shut it behind me.

"Good morning, Bill, nice weekend?" I asked.

"Same as all the others I've had of late. Al Smith's picture was all over the news this morning. What the hell's going on?"

"You better sit down for this one," I said as I took a seat. I then described in detail the weekend that was. I didn't leave out any facts.

I think it impressed Bill when I gave him a synopsis of the case without having to review notes. I gave him all the pertinent details and left out the window dressing. When I finished, I saw Bill as I had never seen him before. Speechless. Well...for a moment anyway.

"So the way you tell it, every lead has hit a brick wall, and you're right back where you started," he said. "You have no more of an idea who is behind these fires now than you did when the first one was reported."

"True," I replied.

"The only progress has been the cigarette angle, which led to Al Smith and possibly the Mitchum family, which is pretty flimsy in its own right as you only found out that the Mrs. smokes that kind of cigarette. You have no evidence to support a theory of the Mitchum's being possible traffickers."

"Correct."

There was silence for a moment.

"That notion about Mike is disturbing," he said.

"Yes, it is. I haven't had a chance to think it all through yet, but it does warrant a great deal of concern."

"Well then give it some thought, man! Let me help you!"

I couldn't wait to hear what he had to say next.

"Let's hypothesize for a moment. Let's say Mike wanted in on the action. I know for a fact he tried to bring down one of the head honchos of the trafficking operation and was unable to do so. Lack of evidence coupled with the disappearance of the few witnesses saw to that. So what if he was of the opinion 'if you can't beat them, join them'? How could he infiltrate the market? How could he when all the territories were already looked after? Knocking off one of the head boys would create an opening now, wouldn't it. But Mike is pretty subtle. First, he may try to become partners with one of the big boys, and when that failed...well, we can't ask Al Smith what he would do given such a predicament because he's lying on a slab in the morgue.

"Let's also say somebody stumbled onto Mike's plan, and he found out about it. That certainly wouldn't do. He'd be stopped before he even got started. So how would you make a death look like an accident? For that matter, why bother having to deal with a death when a mere disappearance would take care of the problem. Maybe start a few fires to throw the insurer's investigation into turnaround, or have someone else start the fires. No need to put yourself at any more risk than was necessary. I'm just thinking aloud, you understand."

"Right, sure, of course" was all I could muster.

"Gives one pause for thought, doesn't it?"

"Let me ask you, Bill, have you ever given any thought to entering the investigations field?"

With a smile (and I have never seen Bill smile) he said, "I'm just thinking aloud, that's all."

"How do you know Mike tried to bring down the contraband smoke ring? I don't remember seeing that on the news or in the newspaper," I said.

"You wouldn't have seen nor heard anything about it. It was kept strictly hush-hush. The big brass of the police department were the only ones in the know, one of them being a friend of mine," he said.

"Get back to me when you've made some progress. I have a conference call to make. Please shut the door on your way out."

CHAPTER TWENTY- ONE

Surveillance

As we left the office building, I couldn't help wondering what other insights Bill might be coveting. He certainly formulated the plot revolving around Mike very quickly.

"What happened in there?" Jesse asked.

"I gave Bill all the facts. He thought them over and asked me to report back when I've made some progress. He also thought the cigarette angle was interesting," I replied.

"So what's next?"

My Blackberry started ringing before I could reply.

"Hold that thought lad," I said. "Samuels."

"Hi Trevor, it's Tracy. Sorry to bother you, but I can't get a hold of the Lipton's, and I need to review the construction agenda with them. Maybe they're still sleeping. Do you know what time they got back to the motel last night?"

"It's no bother at all. I just got out of a meeting with Bill. Was bringing him up to speed on the case. It turns out the Lipton's were out looking for Jesse. They got back around 2:00 this morning. They're probably still sleeping."

"That's what I figured. They must've been relieved to get Jesse back safe and sound."

"Yes, they certainly were. I think he'll will be grounded for the next few weeks though."

"If he were mine, he would be. I'll wait for a few hours and try the Lipton's again. Thanks for the info, I'll talk to you later."

"What the fuck was that all about?" Jesse asked after I ended the call.

"It was Tracy. She's been trying to get in touch with your parents."

"Oh. Why did you tell her they showed up at the motel last night?"

"Because I didn't want to tell her they've disappeared. Only divulge what you have to until you're certain it's safe to give out all of the details. That's rule one when it comes to investigating."

"...Right," he said. "So what's our next step?"

"I think you're right," I said.

"Of course I am...about what?"

"About Al being taken out so someone could take over his territory."

"Okay, but who?"

"I've been giving that a lot of thought. The only name that keeps recurring is Mike's."

"MIKE? The cop? Did you fall on your head or something?"

"There are a lot of loose ends when it comes to Mike, smart-ass. I want those loose ends tied up."

"Like what?"

"For starters, why didn't he put any yellow crime scene tape around the perimeter of your house after the fire? That's standard police procedure. Secondly, where did he get my cell phone number? I never gave it to him, and it's not listed in any directory. Thirdly, why did he text me when you went missing? It would have been a lot easier if he had called to let me know. And most importantly, why didn't he ask about possible motives for your parent's disappearance and Al's killing? He never asked me why someone would kill Al or take your parents. A lot of things don't add up."

"Interesting," he said.

"Isn't it though. Anyway, I don't want to confront Mike about all this. He may think I suspect him. I certainly don't want him putting his guard up if he is involved."

"That makes sense. So what are we gonna do?"

"Rent a car and follow him. We have to be careful though. He's trained to spot people tailing him."

"Cool. Can we rent a Ferrari?" Jesse asked with a smile on his face.

"Oh sure, a Ferrari wouldn't attract any attention. I'm sure Mike would never even notice us."

"Now who's being a smart-ass?"

I rented a Hyundai Accent from a local rental agency. It was a little small, but it was the only car they had available. Nothing like no choice to help you make up your mind. Jesse and I were parked a block away from the police station. The unmarked Ford Crown Victoria Mike always drove was parked outside the front door.

"Now what?" Jesse asked.

"Now we wait."

"Bor-ring."

"You think surveillance work is all car chases? Think again. Most of the time you just sit and wait for your subject to move."

We sat in the car for an hour before Mike came out the front door and got into his car. I waited a few seconds after he left before pulling away from the curb. I tried to stay four or five car-lengths behind him at all times. I didn't want to get too close nor fall too far behind. He drove out of downtown Malone and headed west along County Road 10. I thought he may have been heading to Windham Estates, a posh little sub-division just outside Malone that catered to the wealthy upper class. The entire sub-division was comprised of ten homes, the smallest being five thousand square feet. Some of the homes had indoor pools while others had tennis courts and outdoor hot tubs. I saw Mike's left signal flash. He was definitely heading to Windham. With traffic, I couldn't immediately turn to follow him.

His car was nowhere to be seen by the time I turned onto Windham Terrace, the only street leading to this little slice of heaven.

"Keep your eyes peeled," I said.

"I'm watchin'," Jesse replied.

We drove slowly down the street. I was watching the left side of the road while Jesse watched the right.

"There," Jesse almost screamed.

The Crown Vic was parked in the driveway of the last house on the right hand side of the street. I stopped the car when we were three houses away and looked around. I caught sight of the mailbox across the street from the house; it had "ROGERS" stenciled along its side.

How the hell could Mike afford such an extravagant house? I know police chiefs were paid well, but not this well. His house was a two story, red brick masterpiece. The concrete porch leading to the double front doors was bigger than my driveway! The porch cover was supported by huge wooden pillars, and the triple car driveway was constructed of interlocking brick. Every window on the second floor had a balcony. The house had to be at least ten thousand square feet, and Mike was single! This certainly gave me pause for thought.

"Holy fuck! Look at his house!" Jesse said.

"Yes, it's certainly impressive, isn't it," I replied.

"Do cops make six figure salaries? Where do I sign up?"

"No, they don't. He obviously has money coming in from another source. Maybe an inheritance?"

"Bullshit. He's dirty, and you know it."

"Don't jump to conclusions, lad. Let's see where he goes next."

We sat there for three hours. The neighbors must've been wondering what we were doing.

"Okay, I think he's staying home tonight. We'll come back early in the morning," I said as I started the car.

"But what if he goes somewhere?"

"It's a chance we have to take. We can't sit out here all night. The neighbors will call the cops, and Mike will be the first to respond."

"That fuckin' sucks," Jesse said.

I looked at him and asked, "Has your mother ever washed your mouth out with soap?"

He turned to me and replied, "Yeah, but it didn't do any fuckin' good."

CHAPTER TWENTY- TWO

The Reserve

We were back on Windham Terrace at 4:00 morning. Jesse was sleeping in the backseat while I nursed a cup of coffee from my thermos. It might be Spring, but it was still damn cold in the early mornings.

Even though Mike owned the last house, the street itself continued. Instead of stopping before we reached Mike's house, I continued passed it, turned around, and parked on the side of the road. This way Mike wouldn't see us when he left for work. Unless he drove down the street in this direction. Being the lone car on a desolate stretch of road, if he saw us, he'd know something was up.

Lucky for us, we didn't have to wait in the cold very long. At 4:30, Mike walked to his car. He backed out of his driveway and headed back the way he had entered the night before. There's no way he was heading to work at this hour, not unless an emergency had arisen.

Once his taillights had disappeared from view, I started the rental and headed down the street. I could see the faint outline of his car when I turned right onto County Road 10. I kept back to ensure his suspicions didn't get aroused. Just when I began to think he was heading to his office, his left turn signal flashed. He was heading for the highway.

We followed about ten car-lengths behind him. Too bad he left so early. There wasn't much traffic to conceal us. Half an hour into the journey, I began to wonder where he was going. Fifteen minutes later, he took the off-ramp leading to the Matapon Indian Reserve. Why would Mike be headed to an Indian reserve? I wondered. Only one reason popped into my mind: Mike was one of the kingpins. He had to be. All of the fires took place in one territory, the one serviced by Jesse and supplied by Al. I'd bet a year's salary Mike was the kingpin of this territory.

Mike disappeared into the reserve. I didn't want to attract attention, so I pulled into a diner down the street and parked the car. I made sure the car was facing the reserve, so I could watch for Mike. I wanted to wake Jesse so I could tell him of this development, but then I remembered how grumpy he was in the morning. Best to let him sleep.

Almost an hour later, I saw a white cube van pull out of the reserve and head this way. Mike's car was right behind it, but he headed in the direction of the highway. He must be going back to the city. I crouched down in my seat so the driver of the cube van wouldn't see me when he drove by. Instead of driving by, however, the van stopped on the side of the road and the driver got out. He must be getting some coffee from the diner. I kept my eye on the side view mirror. Luckily, the parking lot was well lit. When I got a look at the driver, I almost screamed. It was Betty Smith.

Betty was the courier. I just sat there, crouched low in my seat, trying to digest this latest development. Mike was the kingpin,

Betty the courier, Al had been the supplier, and Jesse one of the sellers. The hierarchy was complete. That nervous breakdown Betty suffered must have been an act, and a damn good one. She would've had to convince every police officer on the scene of Al's killing. Mike undoubtedly knew it was an act. He probably put her up to it.

I was still reeling when Betty came back out of the diner with a coffee in her hand. She got back into the truck, did a three point turn, and headed in the direction of the highway. I started my car and pulled out about a minute after she started to drive away. I saw her take the on-ramp to the highway. She must be taking a shipment to the city. If I played my cards right, I could find out where the stock was being stored.

We were almost back to the city when I heard Jesse begin to stir in the backseat. I brought him up to speed on the morning's events as soon as he sat up. He didn't say a thing until I finished the story.

"Holy shit!" he said.

"You can say that again," I replied.

"You don't get it. If Betty's in on it, she'll know about my debt to Al. She's gonna come lookin' for me," He said in a panic.

"I doubt that's foremost on her mind right now. She's just a driver. She may not even know about your debt. And even if she does know about it, she'd never try to collect. Her cover would be blown. I think your safe for now, at least until they hire another supplier to replace Al."

"Yeah, I guess that makes sense."

Betty veered onto the off-ramp that led to County Road 10. It suddenly dawned on me: where could you hide a load of cigarettes that took a cube van to transport? A ten thousand square foot house. As if on cue, her left turn signal light flashed at the corner of Windham Terrace. No need to follow her any further. I knew where she was going.

Mike was a kingpin. I couldn't believe it. He'd obviously done very well, given the size of his house and all. He'd obviously been involved with the trafficking operation for quite some time.

As we headed home, I realized I hadn't paid my respects to the widow Smith. It seemed only proper that I check in and see how she was doing. She must be home from the hospital by now. No doubt she had a miraculous recovery. Jesse's sarcasm must've been rubbing off on me. I wanted to see how Betty would react when I showed up at her house.

I spent the rest of the morning reviewing my files. Jesse played fetch with Casey, then took him for a walk. After lunch, I took a nap for a few hours. I awoke to find Jessie asleep on the living room couch. I figured it was safe to leave him for a bit, so I headed out to the Smith homestead.

I arrived at 4:00 p.m. The sun was shining and the day had warmed up considerably. I parked beside the front porch and walked to the front door. The door opened when I was about to ring the bell. Thomas Smith stood on the threshold with a look of surprise on his face. I must've startled him.

"Sorry about that, I didn't mean to scare you. I was about to ring the bell," I said.

"Oh, no problem, I was just on my way out. Can I help you?" he replied.

"I'm Trevor Samuels. I think we met the night of the fire?"

"I remember you. My mom's not here right now. I'm not sure when she'll be back."

"I'm sorry about your father."

"Thanks."

"I can't even imagine having that much bad luck."

"What do you mean, sir?"

He was a polite kid.

"Well, first you suffer the loss of everything you own in a fire. Then you lose your father. Must be very traumatic for all of you."

"It's hard, but we'll manage. It was a weird scenario though."

He seemed like a mature kid, too.

"What do you mean?" I asked.

"My mom, sister, and I were staying over at my grandparents house on the night of the fire. Dad wanted to stay home."

"Is that right?"

"Yes, sir. That wasn't a surprise though. He never liked my mom's parents. He never came with us when we visited them."

"So what was weird then?"

"Well, he told my mom he was going to stay home because he wasn't feeling well. We were afraid he was in the house when it burned to the ground. But he wasn't. He had gone out to an all-night poker game."

"Had he now. Did he do that often?"

"Not often, maybe once a month."

"So a poker game saved his life."

"Yes, it did. That's what I mean about being weird. He escaped death once, but not twice."

"That's quite the story."

"Yeah. Anyway, I have to go. I'll tell my mom you stopped by."

"No worries. I'll stop by to pay my respects another time. Take care, Thomas."

"You, too, Mr. Samuels."

    I tried to connect the events of this day with what I had learned over the past four days. The Mitchum's had a fire. Their fire didn't seem to tie into the latter two. Someone set fire to the Smith house when Al was thought to be home alone. Except he wasn't home. Why would someone want to kill Al? To take over as Mike's supplier? Perhaps. It was time to bring forward some facts from the back of my mind.

Al was arrogant. Al was an asshole. Al loved money. What if Al wanted a bigger piece of the contraband pie? What if Mike didn't want to pay him more money? What if Mike tried to solve the problem by burning down the Smith house with Al inside? What if Al knew Mike had tried to kill him by burning down his house? Mike would have to resolve the problem very quickly. Guns offered quick resolutions.

It was all starting to come together. Betty was the only piece that didn't fit. Unless, of course, she wasn't happy. Maybe her marriage was failing? I wouldn't be surprised given Al's personality. Was Betty the sole beneficiary of Al's Estate? Perhaps this was her way out. Maybe Mike would promote her from courier to supplier? Suppliers made more money than couriers. The more I thought about it, the more this piece began to fit.

CHAPTER TWENTY- THREE

Theft

How could I get inside information on the cigarette trafficking operation? How could I infiltrate Mike's world and bring him down? I had a few ideas but only one really stood out.

"Are you fuckin' crazy?" Jesse asked over a bowl of cereal.

"What?" I replied.

"You can't steal Mike's stash! He'll come after you with both barrels!"

"Exactly," I said as I took a bite of my bagel.

"You can leave me out of this one. You're gonna get yourself killed!"

"Not necessarily. What if I wanted to join forces with Mike? What if I'd been trying to think of a way to get involved in the "business"? What if I thought no one would take me seriously? I'd have to do something to make them think otherwise. Can you think of a better way to turn his head?"

"Not really. But how are you gonna break into his house and steal them? Don't you think he has an alarm on his house? And, in case you hadn't thought of it, not many cases will fit in your car."

"No, I don't think he has an alarm on his house. Why would the police chief need an alarm on his house? That wouldn't instill a lot of confidence in the citizens of his city. I can see the headline now - Malone Police Chief Alarms House. He doesn't have any confidence in his staff and is worried about rampant crime in the area. That wouldn't be a pretty situation, Jesse. As for breaking into his house, that's where you come in. You picked my lock. I'm sure you can pick his, too."

"Me? I already told you I'm not getting involved in this."

"Now, Jesse, what happened to your sense of adventure? Everything will work out in the end, you'll see."

"Uh huh. And what about the car?"

"That's easy. I'll rent a cube van. We'll bring the smokes back here, and I'll think of a way to tip Mike off that I have them. Piece of cake."

"Have you given any thought to finding my parents?" he asked out of the blue

"I'm still working on that. I think the answer will present itself in due time. I'm sure their whereabouts will become known as the case progresses. Their disappearance has to be tied to this case."

He sat there quietly eating his cereal.

I watched the local noon news and found out that Mike was going to be in court all day. He had to testify against someone accused of breaking and entering. I hadn't planned on breaking into Mike's house today, but since I knew he wouldn't be home... well, why waste the day.

I rented a cube van, and we drove to his Windham Terrace home. I backed the cube van into the driveway and took my lawn mower and weed whacker out of the back. I wanted the neighbors to think we were there to cut the lawn. I pushed the mower to the back of the house while Jesse followed with the weed whacker. We ditched the lawn care equipment as soon as we reached the backyard. There were no houses behind Mike's, so we had some privacy. We headed for the back door.

"Try to hurry," I said to Jesse as he took out his lock pick.

"I'll work as fast as I can. These are better locks than you have on your doors, you know."

"I don't doubt it. Who taught you to pick locks anyway?" I asked as he began to work the lock

"A friend of mine. I figured it would come in handy some day."

"You were right," I said with a smile.

With a click, Jesse turned the doorknob, and we walked in.

"That didn't take long," I said.

He just smiled.

"Okay, let's search the house. We'll start in the basement."

"Shouldn't we spread out? That way it won't take as long to search the house."

"No. What if someone comes home? I don't want us to be at opposite ends of the house."

As luck would have it, the basement stairs were right by the back door, just where they should be. God only knows where they would have been if this was Al's house. I silently hoped we'd have to search the whole house. I'd love to see the expensive furnishings Mike surely had.

At the bottom of the stairs, we entered a room as big as the first floor of my house. It looked to be an exercise room. There were athletic machines everywhere. I saw a door at the far end of the room and instructed Jesse to check it out. I wanted to check out the door on the wall to our right. It looked like one of those commercial freezer doors. It also looked a little out of place in here. When I got to the door, I noticed a temperature dial on the frame. It read -30.

I'll be damned. It was a freezer. And a very cold one at that. I pulled the handle until the door opened a quarter of the way into the basement. I didn't need to open it any further. The bodies of Peter & Marsha Lipton were lying on the floor! They were face up and frozen solid. I quickly shut the door and leaned against it while I tried to catch my breath.

"Jackpot!" Jesse yelled as he ran toward me.

"Huh?"

"I found them. There's gotta be over a thousand cases in there! There's no way we can get them all out of here. There's at least two truckloads' worth. What's wrong with you? You look like you've seen a ghost."

"Nothing, it was just damn cold in there."

"What's in there? Can I look inside?"

"No, there's nothing in there," I said with my back leaning against the door.

"Come on, let's get started. We have to get out of here," I said as I ushered him back toward the far door.

A thousand cases was right! They were everywhere. I didn't have the time to stand around and absorb the moment.

"Come on, let's go!" I said to Jesse.

We started carrying the cases into the garage. Luckily, the door to the garage was at the top of the stairs. It was better than carrying them one by one around the back of the house to the van. After half an hour, we were both sweating. We had moved about 200 cases into the garage. One fifth of his inventory. He'd definitely notice them missing. As we were catching our breath, Jesse said, "Can I sell four cases? I can get the money to pay Betty Smith."

"No, you can't sell four cases. They're not ours."

"Come on, he won't notice four cases out of a thousand."

"Trust me, Jesse, he'd notice. Criminals always notice when somebody rips them off."

"What if something happens, and we end up keeping the cigarettes?"

"The cigarettes might be needed as evidence at Mike's trial. Besides, I intend on bringing down everyone involved in this case. That includes Betty. She can't collect from you if she's behind bars."

That seemed to satisfy him.

"Okay, I'm going to open the garage door and the back door of the cube van. As soon as I do, start throwing the cases as far as you can. That way we won't have to stop to push them further into the truck."

And with that, we started. Cases were flying left and right. I took a quick look around. I couldn't see anyone watching, but you never know. We had to move quickly. After the cases were loaded, I shut the van door and hit the button to lower the garage door.

We were dog tired by the time dinner hour rolled around. The 200 cases were stacked neatly in my basement, and we had returned the cube van. In the taxi on the way home, I wondered how I should tip off Mike that I had his wares.

I ordered a pizza when we got home. I didn't have the energy to cook. Jesse fell asleep on the couch watching TV after he ate. I couldn't sleep. I couldn't get the image of Peter and Marsha out of my head. Why did Mike have their bodies at his house? Must be temporary until he could figure out where to unload the bodies. He must've taken them from the motel to his house and killed them, or had them killed. Or perhaps he went to see them at the motel and things got out of hand. He might have accidentally killed one of them. Of course then he'd have to kill the other one. he couldn't leave a witness. Maybe then he had them taken back to his house, already dead. But why? Had a member of the Lipton household come across his illegal enterprise? Was he afraid Jesse had found out that he was the kingpin? Doubtful. He would have killed Jesse if that were the case. So what if one of the Lipton's had discovered his secret business? Maybe Peter found out and told Marsha about it or vice versa. If that were the case, they would have to be eliminated. Maybe they had some evidence and threatened to expose him? How would Mike get the evidence? Burning down their house would destroy it. Why wouldn't he make sure they were home at the time of the fire, kill two birds with one stone? That didn't work so well with Al, maybe burning down the house one day and killing them shortly thereafter was a better way to go. Did that make sense? Yes, it did. These were only guesses of course. I had no evidence to support any of these theories. But they made sense to me. Hopefully, I'd be able to prove one or more of these theories eventually. Possibly when the case was near closure.

One thing is for damn sure. My gut instincts were as sharp as they ever were. Could you imagine what would have happened if I had called Mike when I discovered that Al was a supplier? He would have killed me sooner rather than later.

Why didn't Mike ask about possible motives for Al's killing and the Lipton's disappearances? Because he already knew the answers. I was surprised at his sloppiness, however. He still should have asked my opinion as to motives. Maybe he didn't think I was smart enough to notice that he hadn't asked.

Why no crime scene tape at the Lipton's? Sloppy again. Though I am surprised one of his constables didn't mention it to him.

A new question just dawned on me. Why wasn't Jesse ever caught when he was selling his stash at school? He said the kids were lined up at the back of the parking lot after last bell. And this happened regularly. Surely one of the teachers walking to their car after school would have noticed the crowd and looked into it. Yet nothing had ever happened. Maybe he was just lucky?

What was I talking about? I knew the answer! Nothing happened because Mike was the kingpin. He wouldn't bust one of his own sellers. That would be taking money out of his own pocket. Now I was getting sloppy. I had to get some sleep. I needed a clear head tomorrow.

CHAPTER TWENTY- FOUR

The Proposal

I was dozing off in front of the TV when the doorbell rang. I looked at my watch: 10:30 p.m. I wondered who was at the door at this time of night. I was pleasantly surprised to find Tracy standing on the front porch.

"Good evening, come on in," I said.

"Hi, Trevor, sorry about stopping by so late," she said as she crossed the threshold into my dining room. I shut the door behind her.

"No problem. Jesse's sleeping, and I was watching TV. So what brings you to this part of town so late?"

I hadn't noticed the tiny revolver in her left hand until now.

"I think you know why I'm here," she said as she aimed the pistol at my chest.

"Uhm....not really, no," I said while my mind raced to think of a way to separate her from the gun.

"Mike Rogers asked me to drop by and collect what's rightfully his," she said with a broad smile on her face.

"What are you talking about? I don't have anything of Mike's," I said.

"You don't have two hundred cases of his cigarettes in this house?"

"Cigarettes? Why would I have cases of cigarettes?"

"You know, Trevor, for an investigator, you're not very observant. You drove a cube van from Mike's house to this house this afternoon. Betty Smith was driving to Mike's when she saw you pull out of his driveway. She followed you back here. So I ask you again, where are the cases?"

"Why would you get mixed up in something like this, Tracy? You have a good job and earn a decent salary. Why?"

"Decent salary? Working around the clock for a mere $40,000 a year is decent? The government taking 40% of my salary in taxes is decent? Working like a dog and never getting ahead is decent? You know what's decent, Trevor? Tax-free cash and a lot of it, and that's what I'm making now."

I didn't know what to say or do. It appeared I was slightly off the mark when I thought Betty would become the next supplier.

"How long have you been working for Mike?" I asked.

Tracy smiled and relaxed, slightly. "Well, since I know you'll never be able to tell anyone about this," she began, "it's been since the Mitchum fire. That was my initiation. He wanted to see if I could pull it off. I stumbled across Mike's side-venture while I was adjusting a loss last month. I approached him and asked for a job. He was quite surprised. In hindsight, it wasn't very smart of me to approach him.

"He could have killed me right there. He, however, saw value in my job as an adjuster. Who better to work on an arson case than a member of his own team? Especially when that team member had committed the arson! He also mentioned Al was getting greedy and that he would like to have him replaced. I told him I could help him with that so long as I was named his replacement."

"Sounds like you're quite an asset to him."

"I sure am, and in more ways than you realize." She laughed a bit and leaned against the wall; the gun never wavered from its intended target: me.

"Remember when I said the Lipton's statements hadn't provided any new details?" she asked.

I nodded.

"Peter's statement was actually quite interesting. He told me about Jesse returning home the night of the fire. He saw Jesse leave the Parker house and followed him. He also saw Al drop off the cases of cigarettes, though he didn't know they were cigarettes at that point. Peter searched the cases after Jesse had left to return to the Parkers.

"He didn't want to report it to the police as they would arrest Jesse. I told Peter he had to report what he'd seen to Mike. If he didn't, he could also be charged. I also reminded him that Jesse was a juvenile and wouldn't get into much trouble. Probably just some community service. May even do the kid some good. I guess I persuaded him because he called Mike as soon as I left the motel. Mike was very appreciative."

"So you got the Lipton's killed," I said somberly.

"So you did see their bodies in the freezer." She nodded. "We weren't sure if you had or not. Mike and I paid the Lipton's a visit on Saturday afternoon. Good thing Mike owns a cube van. We needed the space. We rolled them in plastic after Mike shot them. He put them in the van, and we took them to his place."

I was speechless. I thought of the TV in the Lipton's motel room. The volume was very high when I turned it on last time I was there. Mike must have cranked the volume to muffle the sound of the gunshots.

"Did you torch the Lipton's house as well?"

"Yeah, but it was just for fun. I got such a rush from the first two. I wanted more!" She closed her eyes briefly, and then opened them. The look on her face was pure bliss. "You have no idea what an adrenaline rush you experience. I can't even describe it. I lost my boyfriend in that fire, too. I told him what a rush the first two were, so he came with me for the third. Too bad the fire got him. He was great in bed."

A huge part of me wanted to lunge for her, grab the gun, and be done with her. But, I stood in front of a crazy bitch holding a gun. I had to remind myself to tread carefully.

"Funny, I had Betty pegged as Al's replacement," I said.

"No way, Betty's far too anxious for that kind of work. She's skittish enough driving the truck. Besides, Al left her well taken care of. He had a million dollar insurance policy on his life, not to mention his other investments. Mike knew she wanted Al out of the picture and proposed the fire. She was all for it. She was shocked when he didn't perish as planned, however. I took care of him the proper way shortly thereafter."

I was about to ask what she intended to do with Jesse and I when the living room blind covering the window facing the street suddenly lashed inward. I also heard the window shatter. Tracy's face went blank as she collapsed in front of me. Not being a homicide investigator, I wasn't used to seeing dead bodies, let alone seeing a person get killed right in front of me. I just stood there in shock. Jesse jumped off the couch and started yelling something while trying to pull me toward the back door. I turned to look at him just as Mike came in the front door.

"Hi, Trev, sorry about your window, but you know how I like to make an exciting entrance," he said as he walked from the dining room to the living room. He kept the pistol in his right hand aimed at my chest. "You stupid bitch," he said while looking down at the pool of blood developing around Tracy's head. He then looked at Jesse and I.

"Can you imagine an employee making demands of her employer? Telling me she was goin' to be my next supplier, constantly bitchin' about the way things should be done. She was driving me crazy!"

"No, I couldn't imagine that, Mike," I replied softly.

"I always knew you were smart, Trev. I didn't think you were smart enough to piece this case together, but since you obviously have, here I am," he said with a smile on his face.

I put my arm around Jesse's shoulders. It was more to steady myself than to comfort him.

"What I need is a smart supplier. Think about it, Trev, all the money we can make. Hell, one of my sellers is already living under your roof! I got to thinkin' before Tracy took out Al about the perfect team. My deal with the reserve is very favorable. Betty has been driving for me for quite some time now. She never creates any problems.

"I have lots of sellers who distribute as many cartons as I can supply. My only weakness was in the supplier position. Al had to be let go as we disagreed on the amount of his remuneration. So I thought to myself, to whom should I offer the job? I thought of you immediately. Not only are you smart, you have the ability to close this investigation right now.

"Tracy torched those three houses after striking a deal with a local contractor. She would convince the homeowners to use said contractor in exchange for a piece of the contractor's payments. Now that someone has killed her, case closed. It's a job for the police now.

"Trev, with your intelligence and my network, the sky's the limit! Think of it, we could establish new networks, broaden our distribution, and maybe even take over another territory. We can be millionaires, Trevor. You can live the life you deserve, not to mention the life the boy deserves. Think of him, he's lost everything.

So what do you think?" Mike said. He had shifted his weight from one foot to the other during the entire spiel he had just laid at my feet. He was obviously nervous as well.

I couldn't believe he was offering me a job. Jesse and I were dead if I turned it down. He wanted me to stop the investigation, but he obviously didn't understand insurance at all. Did he not think Balmoral would investigate my finding that Tracy was crooked? That they wouldn't talk to the contractor she was supposedly doing business with? Mike must have figured Balmoral would report the contractor to the police. He could take it from there, let the contractor off due to lack of evidence. The fact that he believed Jesse could continue selling for him even after learning about his parents' fate stunned me. Mike definitely had arrogance in spades. "That's an interesting proposition, Mike," I said in as calm a voice as I could. "How much money are we talking about? And what about Tracy's body in my living room?"

"There we go. Just as I suspected, everyone has their price. We're talking about more money than you could make in a lifetime of investigating. A minimum of $30,000 a month, all in cash, all tax-free. Never mind about Tracy. I'll take care of her body. You just leave that to me, Trev."

"How can I turn an offer like that down? I'd be a fool," I said while attempting to look at Jesse. He was still sitting on the couch, and he must be livid after hearing all of this. Unfortunately, from where I was standing, I couldn't see him. I was surprised he was being so quiet, he must be scared out of his mind.

Mike had a smile from ear to ear as he approached us with his hand extended.

"Put 'er there, Trev," he said. I didn't want to shake his hand. I didn't even want to look at him.

"So do I start with the 200 cases I already have in the basement?" I asked as I shook his hand.

"Yeah, you bet. That's enough to get you started. Al told me the kid here is good at selling, so you shouldn't have any problems."

"Great."

"Now you understand I'll be keepin' a close eye on you two. It's not that I don't trust you. I just have to be sure we're all on the same page. You wouldn't wanna disappoint me. Evidence linkin' you to poor Tracy's murder could end up in my lap. I'd have to pass it along to the district attorney, of course."

"That's understandable. You won't have any problems with us, will he, Jesse?"

"No, it's awesome," Jesse replied. "I was working toward this anyway. I can't think of a better turn out."

"That's good to hear," Mike said as he holstered his weapon and pulled a wad of cash out of his pocket. "Why don't you two stay at a hotel tonight. The boys'll be here shortly to clean up this mess. I'm sure you don't wanna stay here and watch that."

"Sounds good to me," I said as I took the $100 he handed me. "I'll call the president of Balmoral tomorrow morning and tell him I've solved the case."

"Perfect. Why don't you come to my place tomorrow afternoon around 3:00. You know the address," Mike said. "We can work out all the details about your territory and how to launder the money you collect. You won't believe how easy it is."

"I'll be there," I replied.

I knew he would kill us as soon as the investigation was closed and the media circus that was sure to follow had died down. I hadn't lied to Mike about calling Bill. I would do just that first thing in the morning.

"What are we gonna do?" Jesse asked as we drove to the Prescott Motel. Mike was right. I didn't want to stay at my house tonight, not with a corpse on the carpet. I knew Mike would be bugging my phones while he waited for "the boys". He may even have video cameras installed so he could watch our every move. At this point, I didn't care. All that money sure went to Mike's head; he thought everybody could be bought.

"We're going to a motel. Don't worry Jesse, we'll be fine."

"Mike killed my parents."

"Yeah, he did. I saw them when I opened the freezer door in his house. I didn't know how to tell you."

"I wanna kill him."

"That's a natural feeling, but don't even think of doing anything. Let me handle it. I'm going to make him pay for what he's done, and I know exactly how I'm going to do it."

CHAPTER TWENTY- FIVE

Thoughts

Jesse managed to fall asleep an hour after we got to the motel. Shock kept me from sleeping.

Most of my theories had proved accurate, with the exception of Betty assuming the supplier's role. And Tracy's involvement of course.

I reviewed my facts again, making sure I knew exactly what I would tell Bill. Tracy approached Mike as she knew what he was up to. Mike told Tracy she could join his organization if she killed Al. Tracy tried to kill Al by setting fire to his house. She torched the

Mitchum house for practice and the Lipton house for fun. She shot Al when he didn't succumb in the fire.

Peter found out about the illegal cigarette operation and told Tracy about it when she was taking his statement. Tracy talked him into reporting it to Mike. Mike then killed the Lipton's. I tried to show Mike I could be part of his team by stealing some of his stash. I wanted to dig up dirt that could be used to prosecute Mike and his posse. That was the only way I could think to infiltrate his organization. Tracy showed up at my place to re-claim Mike's smokes. Mike showed up at my place and shot her dead. He offered the supplier's job to me, provided I close the investigation. I accepted the job. I would leave out the part about Betty, it wasn't relevant when you looked at the big picture. It was more of a side-story.

At least one more of the questions I had stashed in the back of my mind had been answered. I couldn't figure out how Mike had gotten my cell phone number. Now I knew how: Tracy. . She had obviously given him my address as well.

Sunrise made its appearance at 7:30. Jesse was still asleep, and I had just gotten out of the shower. I grabbed us some fresh clothes before leaving the house last night. I would call Bill as soon as I got dressed. I couldn't wait to hear his thoughts on this one.

True to form, Bill was already behind his desk when I called. I brought him up to speed on everything that had transpired since our last meeting. It would be an understatement if I said he was shocked, especially about Tracy. I voiced a couple of my opinions on how I thought I could nail Mike and his troops to the wall. Bill had a better idea.

CHAPTER TWENTY- SIX

The Wrap Up

I closed the case at 1:00 on this sunny Thursday afternoon. Jesse and I had been riveted to the TV for the last half hour.

After talking with Bill, I went to get Jesse and me some breakfast. Jesse awoke upon my return. As we ate, I filled Jesse in on Bill's idea. We crossed our fingers and, sure enough, Bill came through for us.

One thing stuck in my mind from my conversation with Mike last night. He wanted to expand his business, open new networks and broaden his distribution channels. Most importantly, he wanted to take over another territory. The other kingpins would be very interested in that statement. I told Bill as much and asked if he had any thoughts. He said he did. He also said he'd make a couple of phone calls.

And Jesse and I sat, unable to turn from the TV as we watched the results of Bill's help unfold. A half-hour before one in the afternoon, a breaking news story interrupted normal TV viewing. Mike Rogers, beloved Police Chief of Malone, had been shot and killed at his home. A woman they identified as Mrs. Betty Smith was also killed. She was thought to be his lover. They didn't have any suspects at this point, but a large quantity of contraband cigarettes were found on the premises. A quick check of Mike's active cases didn't turn up any leads; apparently, he wasn't working on any cases having to do with the illegal trafficking of cigarettes.

I called Bill.

"Did you happen to catch the breaking news, Bill?" I asked.

"Yes, I did. Isn't it the damndest thing?" he replied.

"It sure is. I wonder who did it and why."

"I have a theory on that. It's just me thinking aloud you understand."

"Of course, Bill. What's your theory?"

"What if Mike was a kingpin for the distribution of illegal cigarettes in one local territory? What if he wanted to expand his territory? I don't think the kingpins of the other territories would be impressed with that. Especially since it would be one of their territories he would attempt to take over.

"What if Mike's ambition were divulged to the kingpin of the largest territory? I'm sure that man would want to put a stop to any takeover attempt before it had a chance to start. Furthermore, he could grow his own territory by taking over Mike's. What do you think of my theory, Trevor?"

"What can I say, Bill, I'm in awe. I don't know how you come up with these ideas. It certainly sounds feasible. The unfortunate part is we may never find out the truth. The motive for Mike's death may never be found. Not to mention the death of the woman. She was probably just at the wrong place at the wrong time."

"That's very true. We may never find out what really happened."

EPILOGUE

Three Days Later

I slept for two days after hearing of Mike's demise. So did Jesse for that matter.

On a sunny Saturday morning, I sat on my back porch, sipping a hot, freshly brewed coffee. Casey was chasing himself around the backyard. I could watch him frolic all day.

Even though the case was closed, I still couldn't get it out of my mind. There were so many questions left unanswered, like what was going to happen to Thomas and Jessica Smith? Who stole the two hundred cases of cigarettes out of my basement yesterday? Why did Mike text instead of call me when Jesse was missing? Will

Tracy's body ever surface? These questions would never be answered, and I suppose they'll slip to the back of my mind in time.

I heard the screen door open. I looked to my right and found Jesse standing on the porch. He was shielding his eyes from the bright morning sun.

"Good morning," I said.

"Morning."

"All slept out?"

"I think so. What are you doing out here?"

"Just watching Casey run around, and I was thinking about the case."

"Speaking of the case, I have to ask you something."

"Go ahead."

"Well, my parents are gone, and I don't have any other family. What's gonna happen to me?"

READER PARTICIPATION

Thank you for taking a few hours out of your life to read my novel. I hope you enjoyed reading it as much as I enjoyed writing it. As a token of my appreciation, I would like to give you, the reader, the opportunity to direct the course of the third Trevor Samuels mystery. Have you ever wanted a novel to go in a certain direction? Yelled out loud at an author when he or she veered off the path you thought was the best way for the story to go? Well here's your chance to have some input! Trevor Samuels has a website, http://geocities.com/samuelstrevor/index. There's a link on the website that will let you vote on Jesse's future. You can vote "Yes" to keep him involved after the next journey, or you can click "No" to have his involvement removed. The majority wins! I'll keep the website voting open for three months after the publication of this book. Don't be shy!

You can also share your comments on this book. Simply click on the "Comments" link in "The Back of My Mind" micro-site on the website and let me know your thoughts.

PAIN, the second Trevor Samuels Mystery, will be published shortly, and I have begun drafting two versions of the third Trevor Samuels mystery. Only you can decide which draft makes the final cut!

SP

March 24, 2008